D1433037

Love's Surprise

Johnnie Alexander

AnniesFiction.com

Books in The Inn at Magnolia Harbor series

Love's Surprise
Copyright © 2020, 2021 Annie's.

Library of Congress-in-Publication Data
Love's Surprise / by Johnnie Alexander
p. cm.
I. Title
2019956956

AnniesFiction.com
(800) 282-6643
The Inn at Magnolia Harbor™
Series Creator: Shari Lohner
Editor: Lorie Jones
Cover Illustrator: Bonnie Leick

10 11 12 13 14 | Printed in South Korea | 9 8 7 6 5 4 3

Grace

With practiced strokes, Grace Porter maneuvered her kayak alongside the only other watercraft braving the chilly waters of Lake Haven and faced its handsome occupant.

Spencer Lewis tapped Grace's kayak with the end of his paddle. "Don't come any closer," he warned with a grin. A frigid gust tousled his salt-and-pepper hair. "I don't want to go for a roll."

"Is the lake water too cold for you?" Grace teased.

"Too cold for a swim."

"You're the one who wanted to come out here." So far, Grace had managed to stay mostly dry. An experienced kayaker, she wore sturdy shoes, a dry suit and life vest, and waterproof gloves. But her cheeks and the tip of her nose felt like ice cubes. "An 'unseasonable adventure.' Isn't that what you said?"

Spencer laughed, a delightful sound that warmed Grace clear to her toes.

"Using my words against me, are you?" he said. "You have to admit that being out here with no one else around is awe-inspiring. Even humbling."

"First you're an adventurer, and now you're a philosopher. Would the real Spencer Lewis please stand up?"

"Not in this kayak," Spencer retorted.

"And a comedian."

They both laughed.

While Grace paddled away from him, she realized that he was right. The lake's calm waves shimmered beneath the February sun as it descended toward the horizon. The snap in the frosty air meant most people were snuggled up indoors. Smoke rose from nearby chimneys, including the one at the Magnolia Harbor Inn.

The two of them, alone on the deep water, seemed suspended between the blue expanse of the wide lake and the blue expanse of the even wider sky. She closed her eyes and lifted her face to the cold sun, embracing even the uncomfortable aspects of the day's beauty.

Grace still wasn't sure how or why she'd let Spencer talk her into getting the kayaks out of storage. Not that she had protested too much—only enough to sweeten his victory when she finally said yes. His enthusiasm for unusual exploits, such as a paddling stint on the lake in forty-degree weather, was only one of the many things she appreciated about him.

Though she would draw the line at ice diving. Thankfully, he had never suggested that. At least not yet.

A series of barks—high-pitched yaps mingling with deeper ones—sounded from the shore behind her. Grace steered a one-eighty, then waved. Her adorable shih tzu mix, Winston, romped along the bank with Bailey, Spencer's chocolate Lab. Bailey appeared ready to jump into the lake at any minute.

Behind the dogs, Grace's sister, Charlotte Wylde, motioned for them to come ashore, and her boyfriend, Dean Bradley, waved a large silver-plated thermos above his head.

"We're being summoned," Grace called to Spencer as he closed the gap between them.

"What do you suppose Dean has in that thermos?" he asked.

"As long as it's hot, I don't care."

"Race you to shore," Spencer said as he sped past her.

"No fair!" Grace gave it her all, exerting muscles that hadn't been called on for this kind of exercise in months. But Spencer's lead widened despite her effort.

By the time she reached the dock, he was out of his kayak and wrapped in a blanket Charlotte had brought with her. Bailey bounced around Spencer's feet until she received a few pats. Meanwhile, Dean held Grace's kayak steady while she slid onto its rim and then to the dock.

"How was the water?" Charlotte asked, an amused twinkle in her dark-brown eyes.

"It was fine." Grace removed her life vest, then rotated her shoulders. "But that was quite the workout. I'll pay for it in the morning."

Charlotte glanced at Spencer, who was helping Dean bring the kayaks ashore, then placed a flannel blanket around Grace's shoulders. "Worth it, though, right?"

Grace adjusted the blanket and pulled it tight in front, clasping the open ends with one hand. She sneaked a peek at Spencer only to catch him gazing at her.

He immediately turned his attention to Dean and the large thermos.

"Worth it," Grace agreed.

The four settled into Adirondack chairs with mugs of hot chocolate that Dean poured for them and fresh-from-the-oven brownies. Bailey reclined near Spencer's chair, her tail giving an occasional thump as she kept vigil.

As soon as Grace arranged the warm blanket over her lap and legs, Winston jumped into the chair. She rubbed his soft brown ears and gave a contented sigh. The hot chocolate, spiced with cinnamon, warmed her from the inside, and the delicious fudge of the brownie practically melted in her mouth. Nothing could be better than the life she and Charlotte had carved out for themselves since opening the Magnolia Harbor Inn. She wouldn't trade moments like this for anything.

The shadows lengthened, and the air grew chillier as the sun painted the horizon with broad swathes of deep purple, gold, and orange. The majestic colors were reflected in the depths of the lake water as the sun dipped from sight.

They spoke in hushed voices, as if wary of breaking the serene spell that had been cast over them.

As much as Grace wanted time to stop, the moment couldn't last forever. Night was coming.

"Those kayaks won't put themselves away." Spencer rose from his chair and stretched.

Bailey stood beside him.

"I'll help you with them," Dean said, then took Charlotte's hands and pulled her to her feet. "How about popcorn and a movie at your place?"

"I can't believe you're hungry," Charlotte teased. "We almost didn't have any brownies for Grace and Spencer because of you."

Dean shrugged. "What can I say? I like to eat."

While Charlotte and Dean bantered, Grace folded the blankets.

"Thanks for joining me on my unseasonable adventure," Spencer said quietly.

"Thanks for asking me," Grace replied.

"Will I see you at church tomorrow?" He held up a hand. "Wait. It's Charlotte's week to go."

"Yes, and she's singing a solo before the sermon." The sisters took turns attending church so one of them was available at the inn.

"That's great. I always enjoy Charlotte's solos." Spencer scratched the top of Bailey's head and stared at the kayaks resting upside down on the bank.

Why did he suddenly seem uneasy? They'd had a wonderful time on the lake and here at the dock. Had she said something to upset him? She couldn't think of anything. "I can help with the paddles if you want," she offered.

"No need." Spencer glanced toward the other couple, who were discussing what movie to watch. "Dean and I can put everything away." He hesitated, seeming to have more to say.

Grace waited for him to continue.

Instead, he flashed a smile at her, then clapped Dean on the back. "The sooner we put the kayaks away, the sooner you can get that popcorn."

"Let's get it done," Dean replied.

"See you later, Grace." Spencer raised a hand in farewell. He jogged toward the kayaks, and Bailey trotted after him.

When Dean left with Spencer, Charlotte gathered the thermos and container of brownies. She linked one arm through Grace's as they walked toward the inn with Winston on their heels. "Why didn't you invite Spencer to stay? He might have liked popcorn and a movie too."

"He seemed a little distracted," Grace answered. "Besides, we had an especially glorious day on the lake. Sometimes it's best not to drag a good thing out too long."

"I know what you mean." Charlotte tightened her hold on Grace's arm. "You should spend the evening with us. Dean and I can't agree on which movie to watch. You can be the deciding vote."

"No thanks." Grace appreciated Charlotte's invitation, but she didn't want to intrude on the couple's privacy. With their busy schedules, they didn't have much time for leisurely evenings alone. Besides, the physical exercise had worn her out. "I'd probably fall asleep, and then you'd have to carry me home."

"Are you sure?" Charlotte asked.

"Positive." Grace rubbed the back of her neck and winced at the unexpected ache in her shoulder. "I'm going to take a hot shower and get a head start on menu planning. Most of the rooms are booked through Valentine's Day."

"That gives us tomorrow to finalize recipes."

"Winnie is coming over after church to help."

Winnie Bennett was the younger sister of their late mother, Hazel. Their aunt was nearing seventy, but she had the energy of someone half her age. Without Winnie's guidance and support, Grace and Charlotte couldn't have managed the inn as well as they did. She was always available to lend a hand when needed.

"I'll be over as soon as the service ends," Charlotte said. "And I'll bring my famous sweet potato casserole for lunch."

"The one with orange juice and pecans?" Grace asked.

"Shh!" Charlotte put her finger to her lips. "Someone might hear you giving away my secret ingredients."

Grace laughed. "I'm not sure those ingredients are secrets, but I can't wait to eat it. I love that casserole."

They paused when they reached one of the giant magnolia trees that adorned the property. After chatting for a few more moments, Charlotte turned toward her cottage while Grace followed the path to the inn with Winston trotting beside her.

After a quick shower, Grace headed to the kitchen, mentally reviewing how many guests she had for the night. The family of four occupying the Bluebell and Rosebud Suites with their shared bathroom had checked out earlier in the day. The Dogwood Suite guests were sightseeing in Charleston and planned to return late. The two sisters sharing the Buttercup Suite had spent the day antiquing. They'd stopped in around three thirty to drop off a few purchases, then left again with no clear destination in mind.

As Grace poured a glass of water and added lemon slices, she puzzled over Spencer's earlier hesitation and her sense that he had something more to say. Whatever it was, he must have changed his mind.

Grace wished he hadn't.

She placed her planner and Charlotte's menu folder on the kitchen island and perched on one of the upholstered stools. Each hospitality hour this week would have to be extra special for their guests. Grace was mulling over whether to ask Charlotte to bake a four-tiered Black Forest cake or a strawberry cream layer cake when she heard a tap on the window.

Startled, Grace turned.

Spencer grinned at her and played a *rat-a-tat-tat* rhythm on the glass with his fingers.

With a relieved sigh, she motioned for him to come inside.

He rubbed his arms as he entered, Bailey close on his heels. "It's gotten even colder out there."

"Would you like a cup of tea?" Grace asked. "I can put the kettle on." She needed something practical to do. He'd surprised her, and her reaction to his sudden appearance surprised her too. Butterflies crowded her stomach, electricity charged her nerves, and heat pounded her pulse points.

"I can't stay long," Spencer said apologetically. "Megan is on her way home from Chicago, and she's going to give me a call."

Spencer's youngest daughter, a flight attendant with Expedition, lived with Kylie, her older sister, in Charleston. Kylie worked as a physical therapist. The Lewis family was close, and Grace imagined that Spencer's relationship with his daughters had only deepened during their mother's battle with breast cancer many years ago. Grace and Spencer occasionally shared stories about their deceased spouses. About grief and mourning and picking up the pieces of a shattered heart.

"Does Megan still enjoy flying around the country?" Grace asked.

"Loves it," he said. "If there's any truth to some people having a vagabond gene, she's got it in spades."

"Not me." Grace glanced around the kitchen and envisioned all the rooms in the mansion. "I don't think there's anywhere I'd rather be than right here."

Spencer nodded. "Magnolia Harbor is a great place to call home." He ran his hand through his hair and made an odd self-conscious chuckle. "It's been a long time since I've done this."

"Done what?" she asked.

His gaze flitted to the window, the ceiling, and the floor, then landed back on Grace.

Puzzled by his demeanor, she tilted her head and gave him a questioning look. Spencer was usually so calm and direct. Though truth be told, his proximity had her about ready to jump out of her skin. Something had changed between them, but she couldn't pinpoint what.

"I managed to get a couple of tickets to *Les Misérables*." His words came out in a rush.

Grace's eyes widened. "The Broadway show playing in Charleston?"

"The very one."

"But how?" she asked. "Those tickets were sold out months ago."

"I've got connections." Spencer gave her an amused smile. "The tickets are for tomorrow night. Would you do me the honor of accompanying me?"

"I'd love to." Grace smiled. Seeing the Broadway performance of one of her favorite productions was a dream come true.

Spencer visibly relaxed. At least she wasn't the only nervous one. Anyone would think they were teenagers making a date for the senior prom.

"I'll pick you up at five if that's okay," he said. "We can stop and get a bite to eat before the show."

"That sounds perfect," Grace said.

"Great. I'll see you tomorrow then."

She accompanied him to the back door. Despite the chill of the night air, she watched him and Bailey jog toward home until they disappeared in the darkness. Even then, Grace remained at the door, taking in the grandeur of the star-studded sky and the throaty bellows of the lake's nightly orchestra.

She smiled. Nothing could be better than this.

Winnie

Winnie Bennett flipped through one of the cookbooks scattered across the kitchen island at the inn. Two or three were open to pages featuring scrumptious desserts and mouthwatering appetizers. Slips of paper, index cards, and even scraps of ribbon marked pages in others.

"How about berry porridge with rolled oats?" Winnie asked her nieces. "That sounds hearty for a chilly morning."

"I like it." Grace hovered her pen above a pad of paper marked with three headings: *Breakfast*, *Hospitality*, and *Extras*. "I hadn't made up my mind which cake to have—a Black Forest cake or a strawberry cream layer cake—when Spencer startled me last night."

Charlotte straightened as she abruptly closed the lid on her laptop. She stared at her sister expectantly.

"If we do strawberries with the porridge," Grace continued as if she hadn't noticed, "then maybe we should go with the strawberry cream."

"We could also make strawberry scones," Winnie suggested, enjoying the anticipation on Charlotte's face. "And strawberries dipped in chocolate." Those were one of her favorite festive treats. She wouldn't mind if they were served at least once a week at the inn.

Charlotte held up both hands. "Wait a minute."

"Too much strawberry?" Grace asked.

"You can never have too much strawberry," Winnie said innocently. "Especially during the week of Valentine's Day. Though raspberries are nice too."

"Could we forget about food for a minute?" Charlotte asked, glaring at her sister.

"But that's why we're here." Grace tapped the end of her pen on her pad. "To plan the menu."

"And we will," Charlotte said. She sounded exasperated. "But first we need to back up a moment to something you said."

"What did I say?" Grace turned to Winnie with a questioning look.

Winnie shrugged. "Do you prefer the Black Forest cake, Charlotte?" Her niece, an accomplished chef and the author of several popular cookbooks, had decided opinions about food. "Why don't we do both?"

"There's no reason why not." Grace started to write on her pad.

But Charlotte grabbed the pen from her. "Forget the cake." She heaved an exaggerated sigh. "You said Spencer startled you last night. And here I was, feeling guilty all evening because I thought you were alone. I could hardly enjoy the movie."

"Since you were with Dean, I doubt you gave me a second thought." Grace took back her pen. "We have more breakfasts to plan. What else should we have?"

"I thought about you a little," Charlotte said. "Now tell us why Spencer came back."

Winnie rested her hand on Charlotte's arm. "You leave Grace alone now. Maybe she has a reason for not telling us about her evening with Spencer."

"I didn't have an evening with Spencer," Grace protested. "He tapped on the window and scared me. That's all."

"He scared you on purpose?" Charlotte's tone sounded doubtful.

"I don't think he meant to scare me. He simply wanted to know if I'd like to go to Charleston with him this evening." A flush reddened Grace's cheeks. "Now can we finish this so I can get ready?"

"You're going on a date." Charlotte grinned. "I knew it. He's finally asked you on a date. Where are you going?"

"To see *Les Mis*," Grace said. "Can you believe I'm actually going to see it? When I tried to get tickets, they were sold out."

"I'm thrilled for you," Winnie said with genuine enthusiasm. "You'll have such a great time together." As far as she was concerned, Grace and Spencer were spending too much time being just friends. If this was the first step to being more than friends, then Winnie would do whatever she could to see that happen. "Leave the rest of the menu planning to Charlotte and me, and you go get ready."

"You're sweet, but I've got plenty of time." Grace bit her bottom lip. "Besides . . ."

"What is it?" Winnie asked.

Grace paused a moment longer, then smiled at her aunt and sister. "I'm not sure it's a real date."

"Why not?" Charlotte sounded incredulous. "He bought the tickets, didn't he? He asked you, didn't he?"

"But what if he asked because we're friends?" Grace took a deep breath and gave a slight shake of her head. "I don't want to make this into something it's not. I'm going to go and have a good time, and that's it."

"Of course it's a date." Charlotte caught Winnie's gaze and rolled her eyes.

Winnie ducked her head to hide her smile. She loved her sister's daughters as much as her own. She longed for the day when both of them were happily married. Just like her and Gus. She'd been lucky, falling for her high school sweetheart and never regretting one day of their life together. Maybe she should make a special strawberry dessert for him sometime this week. A little reminder of how much he meant to her and how much she appreciated him.

"We're just friends," Grace insisted.

"Methinks thou dost protest too much," Charlotte said as she reopened her laptop.

"Can you handle the hospitality hour on your own?" Grace asked. She clearly wanted to redirect her sister's attention to something else. "Oh, and Justin and Bethany Jett are arriving late this evening too. You'll need to check them in."

"Will do," Charlotte said. "It's not like I'm going to Charleston to see a Broadway musical."

"I'll stick around to help you out," Winnie said. "Are they the only guests checking in today?"

"Unless someone changes their plans, yes." Grace opened her planner and flipped to the current week. "The Jetts are celebrating their fifteenth anniversary. They're staying in the Bluebell Suite. Everyone else arrives tomorrow."

"Who is everyone else?" Winnie enjoyed knowing about the guests before they arrived. Some of them, especially the frequent visitors, had become dear friends.

"Roger and Joy Phillips." Grace checked her notes. "They're newly married and have the Buttercup Suite. And then we have two singles—Trent Jacobs and Presley Ingram. Trent is in Dogwood, and Presley specifically requested the Wisteria Loft Suite."

"I wonder why," Charlotte mused. "Her name doesn't sound familiar. Has she stayed here before?"

"I don't think so," Grace said.

"Where does she live?" Charlotte asked as she tapped on her keyboard.

"New York City," Grace said.

"Here's a picture of her." Charlotte turned her laptop around so Winnie and Grace could see the screen. "This is interesting. She's a fashion designer with lots of awards to her name."

"How can you be sure that's the same person?" Winnie asked.

"This is the only hit for that name in New York," Charlotte replied. "It has to be her."

"She's very pretty," Winnie said, examining the photo on the screen. Something about the woman's name seemed familiar, but she couldn't think why.

"Who's the other single?" Charlotte took control of her laptop again.

"Trent Jacobs," Grace answered. "He's also from New York."

"I wonder if this is him." Charlotte turned the laptop around again to show them another picture. "This guy's a running back for the New York Giants."

"Why would a football player be coming here for Valentine's Day?" Grace asked. "Alone?"

"Maybe because he *is* alone." Charlotte manipulated her screen so that both images appeared side by side. "Look at these two. Wouldn't they make a cute couple?"

Grace laughed, and her blue eyes twinkled. "That's so typical. You're happily in love, and you want everyone else to be in love too. But Cupid might have his own plans for our guests. We should leave them alone."

"I didn't say we needed to set them up on a date," Charlotte protested. "Maybe arrange things so they spend time together. For example, have them sit together at breakfast. That's easy enough, especially since we have two other couples joining us."

Winnie studied the two images. Presley Ingram, styled with sophistication, and Trent Jacobs, decked out in shoulder pads and a rumpled jersey. Both attractive. Both New Yorkers. It might work. Except for one thing.

"We can't be sure they're single," Winnie said.

"Why else would they be coming here alone before Valentine's Day?" Charlotte argued.

"People have all kinds of reasons for coming to the inn, my dear." Winnie poured herself another cup of tea. "After all the guests who have walked through those doors, you should know that." She held up the kettle. "Anyone else?"

"Me," Charlotte said, offering her cup. "But don't think you can distract me that easily. I'm going to do a bit more sleuthing on these two."

"But not now." Grace checked the clock. "We have only one breakfast done and nothing for any of the evening hospitality hours."

"Charlotte and I will come up with the rest," Winnie said as she took Grace's notepad. "We already have a strawberry-and-chocolate theme started, so we can continue with that."

"Great idea," Charlotte enthused. "Go, Grace. Get ready for your big date with Spencer."

"It's not a date," Grace protested, but a smile spread across her face. "Fine. I'll leave you to it."

As soon as Grace was out of the room, Charlotte leaned toward Winnie and lowered her voice. "It's a date."

"Definitely," Winnie said softly. "And it's about time."

3

Presley

The doorbell rang as Presley Ingram placed a zippered bag containing her toiletries in her designer suitcase. She'd pack a few more items after her morning shower, but she needed to be sure the toiletry bag had staked out its own space before she added any more clothes to the suitcase. Deciding which outfits to take shouldn't be this hard. She'd only be gone a week and planned to spend most of her time at the Magnolia Harbor Inn. After all, this wasn't a vacation.

Perhaps it was a mistake to go. What was that saying? *You can't go home again.* Though she wasn't exactly going home.

The doorbell rang once more.

Presley scurried to her apartment's tiny foyer and pushed the intercom button. "Yes?"

"It's Shiloh."

Presley smiled as she opened the door for her best friend. "What a pleasant surprise."

Shiloh Lancour walked inside and greeted her. "Are you all packed?"

"Almost," Presley answered. "Would you like a cup of tea?"

"Sure." Shiloh took off her coat and hung it up on a hook, then set a heart-adorned gift bag on the cushioned bench that sat against one wall.

"Earl Grey or oolong?" Presley asked as they walked to the kitchen.

"I'll take the oolong."

"It sounds like the weather will be fine." Presley put on the kettle, then set out a teapot and two teacups and saucers. "At least warmer than here."

"Maybe I should tag along with you," Shiloh suggested as she perched on a counter stool. "Is it too late?"

"I know you want to be supportive, but I have to do this on my own," Presley said. Everyone needed a friend as faithful and caring as Shiloh. They'd met in their senior year of college when they'd gone on a double date with two guys from the engineering department. The dates were long forgotten, but their friendship had deepened.

"I guess you're right," Shiloh said.

Presley pulled a package of cookies and a plate from the cupboard, then arranged the cookies on the plate. "Once I put the past behind me—for good—then I can make plans for the future. Maybe even make a fresh start. Like you did."

Shiloh had been on her way to stardom as a top model when a drunk driver ran a red light and smashed into her car. The accident had ended Shiloh's career, leaving her with physical scars as a daily reminder of the tragedy. But in time, her indomitable spirit and faith in God had swept away any bitterness. She'd even written the guy a letter saying she'd forgiven him.

During her stints in the hospital, Shiloh had gotten interested in pediatric physical therapy. After her graduation in the spring, she planned to intern at a local children's rehabilitation facility.

"I wouldn't recommend my way of doing it." Shiloh lightened her tone with a gracious smile, but she also rubbed the scar beneath her chin.

Presley suspected the habitual gesture was unintentional. Perhaps it was Shiloh's subconscious way of coping with her tragedy. She'd found forgiveness and her life's calling. But the accident still seemed to hover around her—a specter that would never go away.

"Besides, your career isn't over," Shiloh insisted. "This is only a pothole."

"I'm not so sure about that." Presley reminded herself that her situation wasn't nearly as traumatic as Shiloh's. But its heaviness weighed upon her.

Shiloh opened her mouth to respond.

But Presley held up a hand. "I'm sorry, but I don't want to talk about it anymore." She slid the plate closer to her friend.

"Then let's talk about your trip to Magnolia Harbor," Shiloh said as she helped herself to a cookie. "I looked it up online. The inn is absolutely beautiful. I can't imagine living in a house that big."

"I only stayed there with my grandparents during the summers." *Gorgeous, golden summers.* "It was so different from where I grew up in Chicago."

The kettle whistled, and Presley poured the boiling water into the teapot.

"Has it changed much since you were there last?" Shiloh asked.

"Quite a bit." Presley set the teapot, cups, and saucers on a tray. She had to admit that the two women who'd bought the antebellum mansion—sisters, according to the inn's website—had restored it to a magnificence that had been lacking for decades. "Bring the cookies into the living room, will you?"

Shiloh settled into one of the comfortable upholstered chairs in front of the gas fireplace while Presley set the tea tray on the wooden coffee table. She was known in the fashion industry for her trendy designs, but she preferred a more traditional look for her home.

The chunky walnut bureau and the antique sewing machine that took up way too much space in the small apartment had belonged to her grandparents. Presley had discovered both items in the attic when she was twelve. Grandpa helped her refinish the bureau and hired someone to refurbish the sewing machine.

Grandma hadn't been much of a seamstress, but she taught Presley the basics. That was when her love of working with fabrics, then creating her own designs, had been born. The machine still worked, and Presley enjoyed using it. The rhythmic sound of the treadle set a slow and steady pace she found comforting.

She'd been a junior in college when her grandparents died within a few weeks of each other. Mother had immediately taken control, selling the mansion and everything in it as soon as possible. Presley hadn't attended the estate auction. The thought of strangers pawing through her grandparents' treasured belongings still sickened her. But she'd arranged to purchase the two items without Mother's knowledge.

"I have a few old photographs of the house," Presley said. "If you'd like to see them."

"Absolutely." Shiloh's enthusiastic tone warmed Presley's spirit.

Only her grandparents, especially her genteel grandmother, had loved the mansion more than Presley did. As a teen, Presley had often imagined living there herself someday. Raising her future children in the same place where she had made such happy memories. But that was a pipe dream, made impossible by events out of her control.

Now it was too late.

Mother had never liked living in Magnolia Harbor, but perhaps if the mansion had been in better shape, if it had been one of the premier properties in the area, she would have felt differently. Her mother's trip to oversee the appraisal and the auction was only the second time she'd returned since leaving home as a young woman.

The first time Mother had come back—an involuntary shudder shook Presley's spine. If she relived that humiliation, that nightmare, she might not get on the plane tomorrow.

And she had to get on the plane. She had to go to the inn. She had to find—

"Earth to Presley," Shiloh said, her lighthearted tone barely concealing a tinge of worry. "I thought you were going to show me your photos."

"Sure." Presley managed a weak smile. She retrieved an album from an old trunk that sat beneath one of the large windows. "Here we go."

While sipping their tea and eating their cookies, Presley and Shiloh made their way through the album. The black-and-white photographs in the initial pages depicted her grandparents outside their home. Even though the photos were faded, the signs of neglect of the old place were obvious. Peeling paint. Overgrown shrubs. An overall appearance of weariness.

"My grandmother's parents were wealthy," Presley said. "But the money didn't last. My grandparents managed to hold on to the mansion, but they couldn't afford the upkeep. By the end, they mostly lived on the first floor. They rarely went upstairs. But I did."

Presley flipped a couple of pages to a photo of the exterior of the mansion and pointed to windows on the third floor. "That was my room every summer. It seemed like such a magical place."

"Do you think you'll get to stay there?" Shiloh asked.

"I requested it," Presley said. "They call it the Wisteria Loft Suite."

"I'll bet they're excited to meet a family member," Shiloh said. "But they're probably a little nervous too. Hoping you approve of all the changes."

Presley took a long sip of her tea, her thoughts dragging her back to that last dreadful summer almost ten years ago. The passage of time hadn't removed the sting of her heartache. She set the cup in the saucer harder than she intended, fumbled the china, and placed it on the tray.

"What's wrong?" This time Shiloh didn't try to hide her worried tone.

"The owners don't know I'm a family member."

"Why not?" Shiloh narrowed her eyes in confusion. "I'm sure they'd be delighted to meet you."

"It's better this way." Presley feigned a smile. "I don't want any fuss or hoopla. Just a quiet week to . . . I don't know. Regroup, I guess. Perhaps renew my creative spirit. Seek inspiration."

Shiloh didn't say anything as she leafed through more of the pages, but Presley could sense the tension her friend tried to keep inside. The nervous energy must have built up, though. All of a sudden, Shiloh shut the photo album. "Sometimes I wish the Bible didn't say that vengeance belonged to the Lord."

"I'm not interested in revenge," Presley said.

"But Adriana shouldn't be allowed to get away with taking credit for your work," Shiloh insisted.

"She won't," Presley said with more assurance than she felt. "These things have a way of working themselves out."

"That doesn't mean I wouldn't like to . . . to . . ."

Presley laughed. "You are too good. You can't even come up with something mean."

"Give me time." Shiloh placed the album on the coffee table. "I should go so you can finish packing."

"I'm glad you stopped by. I'll miss you while I'm gone."

They returned to the foyer.

"I almost forgot the reason I came." Shiloh picked up the heart-adorned gift bag from the bench and handed it to Presley. "It's an early Valentine's Day present. Open it."

"But I didn't get you anything."

"Then bring me back a souvenir from Magnolia Harbor."

"You've got it." Presley removed the pink and white tissue paper and took a luxurious leather notebook with a zipped enclosure from the bag.

"It's a travel-size sketch pad," Shiloh said. "It even comes with artist pencils."

Presley unzipped the notebook to reveal thick spiral-bound pages. Two pencils fit in special holders along the inner edges. "This is lovely." The gesture was kind, but Presley didn't intend to do any sketching while she was away. How could she when her creativity was gone? When nothing inspired her?

"I know what you're thinking." Shiloh tilted her head and smiled. "But I also know you. Something will catch your eye. Your fingers will twitch. And if this sketch pad is with you, then you won't have to doodle on napkins or envelopes or whatever scrap of paper you can find."

"I love it." Presley drew her friend into an embrace. "Thank you. For everything."

"I owe you," Shiloh whispered, then put on her coat and hurried out the door.

Presley had only done what any true friend would do during the long months of Shiloh's surgeries and recoveries. Several of Shiloh's other friends hadn't stuck around. They'd intended to, but they had lives of their own to lead, and eventually they'd faded away.

Shiloh had always been appreciative of Presley's loyalty. But Presley wondered if she would have been so attentive if she'd had a family of her own. Maybe then, Shiloh would have had another fading friend.

Presley cleaned up the tea things and put the album away. Before closing the trunk, she pulled out another album and rubbed her hand over the cloth cover.

She shouldn't open it. She wouldn't.

But now that it was in her hands, it was as if she couldn't help herself.

Presley carried the album to the couch, curled up in a corner, and took a deep breath. She allowed herself to indulge in the past—to relive the golden summer moments of her childhood as she and Clint Calloway swam in Lake Haven and went fishing from Clint's skiff. Then there was the tree house nestled within the branches of the climbing tree. The picnics along the lakeshore. The hikes and bicycle rides and the county fair.

Her smile turned to laughter as the photographs reminded her of long-ago memories and the feelings she'd squelched for so long.

A childhood friendship had slowly grown into a teenage crush. By that last summer, Presley and Clint had discovered their feelings were deeper than a crush. They wanted a future together.

They would have had one if Mother hadn't gotten wind of the romance.

"Clint's only a poor country boy," Mother had insisted. "He's searching for any way to break free from the invisible bars holding him in Magnolia Harbor. You're his train ticket out of that swamp. But here's the thing about being someone's train ticket. They're always looking for an upgrade."

When Presley had gotten a little older—a little wiser—she realized that Mother was talking about Presley's father, not Clint. But the realization had done little to heal the hole in Presley's heart. Time had scabbed the wound.

But Mother had torn off the scab in her last e-mail. *That boy you used to play with when you visited your grandparents is getting married. I thought you'd want to know.*

That boy. As if Presley and Clint had still been children when Mother yanked her away.

Mother hadn't bothered to say how she happened to know about Clint's engagement. Presley didn't like to speculate that her mother had been keeping an eye on Clint all these years, ready to pounce if he intruded into Presley's world again.

For her part, Presley had sent a noncommittal reply before doing her own Internet search. The announcement hadn't been hard to find.

She flipped to the back of the album and removed the piece

of paper tucked inside. The printed announcement told of Clint's engagement to an attractive woman with long blonde hair, dimples, and perfect teeth. The epitome of a Southern belle.

Presley covered the woman's face and focused on Clint. The color printout didn't capture the liveliness of his light-blue eyes. The poor guy could barely be out in the sun without a hat and sunglasses. Otherwise, he would get a sunburn.

A small smile tugged at Presley's lips. It seemed every time they were together, Clint had on a different hat.

But those blue eyes shone when he laughed. And he laughed often.

She studied the small lines that crinkled next to his eyes. "I put some of those there," she whispered. But she couldn't be responsible for them now. Someone else had Clint's heart. And Presley only had summertime memories.

Apparently, Mother had been wrong about Clint's desire to leave Magnolia Harbor. Not only was he still there, but he owned his own landscape architecture business. Presley wasn't surprised. He'd always been interested in the historic estates in the area. The run-down properties had fascinated him more than the well-maintained ones. He'd spent hours drawing plans for the gardens at her grandparents' home, though they both knew nothing could ever come of them.

Presley wished she still had the drawings.

Most of all, she wished she had been strong enough to stand up to Mother all those years ago.

4

Grace

The performers bowed to a thunderous ovation, and then the curtain slowly descended onto the stage. The orchestra's final notes resounded through the auditorium before fading away as the lights brightened.

"That was breathtaking." Grace dabbed at her eyes with a tissue. She'd seen the anniversary editions of *Les Misérables* and a couple of the film adaptations. As incredible as she found all those versions, she'd been blown away by the live performance. "This is a night I'll never forget."

"I'm glad you enjoyed it," Spencer said as he escorted her to the lobby. "The staging was superb."

"That part with Javert and the bridge was incredible." Grace recalled the scene when the zealous police inspector, unable to accept the grace shown to him by his nemesis, raised his arm as the bridge rose behind him. It pained Grace to think that anyone could believe death was preferable to life or that grace couldn't be extended without exacting a cost.

But Victor Hugo's classic story also brilliantly showed the power of redemption as Valjean, the convict who stole bread to feed his sister's children, became a respected man who fed the poor and assisted the needy.

"Was that your favorite scene?" Spencer asked.

Grace thought a moment before answering. "It was among the most powerful, and I'm not sure I'll ever forget it. My favorite scene is at the end. It's incredibly sad, of course, when Valjean dies. But it's also full of hope."

"I agree with you," Spencer said. "So many of the songs are stuck in my head. If I could sing half as well as any of those performers, I'd be serenading you all the way home."

"You wouldn't be singing alone."

On the long ride from Charleston to the inn, Grace and Spencer talked more about the Broadway musical. Spencer, who was a retired intelligence analyst for the FBI, mentioned other notable performances he and his family had attended in Washington, D.C., when he was based in Quantico, Virginia.

Eventually, the conversation turned to chitchat about the local news around Magnolia Harbor.

"I suppose next weekend will be busy," Spencer mused. "Since Friday is Valentine's Day, we'll probably have tourists coming to town."

"We usually do have an uptick in visitors this time of year," Grace said. "Then we get a bit of a breather before spring break begins."

"I wonder how hard it is to get reservations at The Tidewater," he remarked. "It'll be a long night for Dean."

Dean co-owned The Tidewater, a trendy inn and restaurant on the other side of the lake. He was also head chef of the restaurant.

"How about your place?" Spencer continued. "Are you already booked solid?"

"We have guests arriving tonight and tomorrow who will be here all week. One couple is on their honeymoon." Grace answered the question as if on autopilot as her mind headed down a rabbit hole. This was Charlotte and Dean's first Valentine's Day together. But Spencer was right. Dean would be busy all evening cooking delicious gourmet meals for his guests. He wouldn't have any time to spare for Charlotte. If only there was something Grace could do for them . . .

"Honeymooners?" Spencer's question broke into her thoughts.

"Yes." Grace smiled as she momentarily flashed back to her own wedding. Wow, the years had flown by since then. But she could still remember the flutters she'd experienced as she said her vows. Her dream of spending a lifetime with Hank had been cruelly cut short by his sudden death, leaving her a young widow with a son to raise on her own.

But these weren't thoughts she wanted to dwell on now. Not when she might be on a date with her handsome neighbor.

"We also have a couple staying with us who are celebrating their fifteenth anniversary," she said to distract her own thoughts from the past.

"Quite a milestone," Spencer said. "What's the traditional gift for that one?"

"Good question." Grace retrieved her phone from her bag and tapped the screen. "This site says crystal. The anniversary gemstone is ruby, and the flower is a rose."

"So a crystal ruby rose would be the perfect gift."

"I suppose you're right. But I don't think that's something I would want."

When Spencer didn't respond, Grace glanced at his profile. His eyebrows were furrowed as if he were deep in thought. Or perhaps he was simply concentrating on driving.

Grace shifted her attention to the landscape beyond the passenger window. There wasn't much to see except ghostly shapes beneath a dark winter sky.

A pall seemed to have settled over both of them. Talk of honeymooners and Valentine's Day could do that. She wished she hadn't brought up the honeymooners and the couple celebrating their anniversary.

"We have two other guests coming too," Grace said, eager to chase away the funk descending on them. "Have you heard of Trent Jacobs?"

Spencer's eyes widened as he glanced at her. "The running back for the Giants?"

"One and the same. At least, we think it's him. We won't know for sure until he shows up."

"I wonder if he's dating someone from Magnolia Harbor," he said. "You wouldn't think a guy like that would be dateless on Valentine's Day, would you?"

"He's handsome enough, I suppose." Grace gave a mischievous smile. "If you're into rugged good looks."

"I'm not sure looks matter when you're a successful athlete like Trent Jacobs. His signing bonus alone probably turned lots of feminine heads."

"Are you saying there are women who would be interested in him only because of his money?" Grace asked, feigning a shocked tone.

"It's a harsh world beyond the borders of Magnolia Harbor," Spencer teased. "I don't want to remove your rose-colored glasses, but not everyone is as kindhearted and honest as you and Charlotte and Winnie."

"I know that's true," Grace said. "But I like my rose-colored glasses, and I intend to keep them."

"And I like them on you." Spencer smiled at her. "It's nice that you still believe the best about people. Even when they disappoint."

Grace's cheeks warmed at the compliment, but she didn't know how to respond. She wanted to tell Spencer that she liked him too. She appreciated his energy, his can-do spirit, and his willingness to lend a hand to anyone who needed it. But she didn't feel comfortable saying any of those things, especially since she wasn't sure of his feelings for her.

After all, Charlotte also believed the best about people. Okay, she hadn't always believed the best about Dean. But that had changed. They made a great couple, and Grace prayed that Charlotte had finally found the man of her dreams. Even though she once might have considered him the man of her nightmares. Fortunately, that was behind them now.

For the rest of the drive, Grace and Spencer sometimes talked and sometimes didn't. But the earlier pall was gone, and their usual comfortable silence seemed to wrap them in a cocoon all their own.

Grace relaxed in that comfort even as she wondered if this was a date or not. But what did it matter? She should simply let herself enjoy her evening with Spencer. She deeply respected him and enjoyed his company. He was a good friend.

A very good friend.

As they neared the inn's drive, Spencer broke the silence. "Do you want to go in the front or around back?"

"Around back, please. Winston may need to go outside, and I don't want to disturb anyone." Grace wondered if Charlotte was waiting up for her inside the inn. She glanced toward the cottage where Charlotte lived. Her home had been a chapel until they bought the property and renovated it. Light appeared through a curtained window, but that didn't mean Charlotte was home.

Spencer parked the car and turned off the ignition. "Sit tight," he said with a grin. Then he hurried around to her side of the car, opened the door, and extended his hand.

"Chivalry isn't dead," Grace teased.

He smiled. "Not when there's a lovely lady around."

Grace returned his smile, took his hand, and stepped from the car.

Spencer placed his hand at the small of her back as they walked toward the back door.

When they reached the porch, Grace pulled her key from her purse. "Do you want to come in for a few minutes? It won't take long to heat up the kettle. Or make a cup of hot chocolate."

"I'd better not," Spencer said. "Besides, I think you've got someone waiting up for you." He smiled and nodded toward the window.

Grace turned just in time to see the curtain fall back into place. "It must be Charlotte. Winston is too short to peek out the window."

Spencer laughed, then shoved his hands into his pockets. "Guess I'll be going."

Grace wasn't ready to say good night. Or for Spencer to leave. But the longer she stood by the door, the more awkward she felt. "It was a wonderful evening. Thanks for asking me."

"We'll have to do it again sometime."

"I'd like that." Grace braced herself, unsure if Spencer meant to kiss her. Unsure of how to respond if he did.

She wanted him to.

She didn't want him to.

Oh, she didn't know what she wanted. All the earlier talk of Valentine's Day and honeymoons and anniversaries had flustered her.

Spencer swayed on the balls of his feet for a moment. When he clasped Grace's elbow, his touch pulsed through the thick wool of her jacket and warmed her skin. "Good night."

"Night."

He nodded, let go of her arm, and returned to his car.

Disappointment settled in the pit of Grace's stomach, but she smiled and waved when he caught her gaze before he headed down the drive.

"I *did* want him to," she mumbled as his taillights disappeared around the curve.

The door behind her slowly opened, and Charlotte joined her on the veranda. She wasn't wearing a jacket so she leaned into Grace and tucked her hands around Grace's arm. "How was it?"

"The food was great, and the production was amazing," Grace said.

"Your first date." Charlotte released an exaggerated heartsick sigh.

It wasn't a date. Just two very good friends sharing an evening together. "You'd better get back inside," Grace urged Charlotte. "You'll freeze out here."

"Aren't you coming in?"

"In a minute."

"I get it," Charlotte said with a teasing lilt. She leaned closer. "You don't want the magic to end."

"Something like that."

Charlotte squeezed Grace's arm and disappeared into the house, leaving Grace alone with her thoughts.

And a heart more confused than ever.

5

Clint

Clint Calloway slid a bite of scrambled eggs through a pool of ketchup while reading the day's edition of the *Harbor Gazette*, a local newspaper. The aroma of strong coffee, sizzling sausage, and freshly baked biscuits filled Aunt Patsy's Porch, the small-town restaurant. The hum of conversation swirled around him along with the clatter of plates and tableware.

"Mind if I join you?"

Clint glanced up at the broad-shouldered man standing by the booth and grinned. "Not at all. Have a seat."

Luke Brannick settled into the bench seat across from Clint. "Don't mean to interrupt your reading."

"Just perusing the local news," Clint said. "Not that there's much new going on in town."

Molly Edwards, the head waitress, stopped by with a coffeepot in one hand and a cup and saucer in the other. "Morning, Luke. Do you know what you want?"

"Guess I'll take the usual. Thanks."

"One usual coming up." Molly placed the cup and saucer in front of Luke, filled the cup with coffee, and topped off Clint's cup with the strong brew before he could stop her.

"Thanks," Clint said. It wasn't a good idea to get on the wrong side of the head waitress, but he could have done without the refill.

When Molly walked away, Luke snorted. "She has a knack for knowing when the coffee is just right, then ruining it."

"Tell me about it." Clint added more cream to his cup and stirred. "What brings you here this morning?"

"Tired of my own cooking. It's not easy being a bachelor." Luke pressed his lips together and momentarily averted his gaze. "Sorry, man. I didn't mean to . . ."

Clint shook his head. "Apologies aren't necessary. It was for the best."

"Still, it can't be easy," Luke said. "I mean, with Valentine's Day coming up. That was supposed to be your wedding day."

"I'm glad it's not. There's too much holiday hype and pretend romance going on this time of year. It's not the date I would have chosen for an anniversary."

"Never made sense to me why women want to get married on that day." Luke stretched his arm along the back of the bench. He'd been a top competitive swimmer in high school, and his long limbs seemed to sprawl away from his body. "Do they expect their husbands to double up on gifts? For Valentine's Day and an anniversary? Seems like it would be better to spread the two apart."

"I'm with you on that one," Clint said.

Molly returned with Luke's breakfast. "Two eggs over easy, hash browns, sausage links, and a stack of silver dollar pancakes on the side with blueberry syrup."

"Looks good," Luke said as he unwrapped the napkin rolled around the tableware.

"It's as good as if I cooked it myself." Molly scanned their table. "Now can I get you two fine gentlemen anything else?"

"Nothing for me." Clint leaned back so Molly could gather his dishes.

Instead, she reached into a pocket and pulled out a wrapped packet tied with a pink and silver ribbon. "We're giving out these sugar cookies for our best customers." She set the packet in front of Clint and pulled out a second packet for Luke. "A special Valentine's week gift from me to you."

"Thanks," Clint said. "That's kind of you."

Molly rested her wrinkled hand on his shoulder. "I know this can't be an easy week for you. But never you mind. That gal doesn't know what she gave up."

Clint simply nodded, afraid that if he said anything, Molly would feel compelled to offer him more of her motherly comfort. When she was out of earshot, he asked, "How is it that everyone remembers I was supposed to get married this week? We canceled the wedding months ago."

"I remembered because I was supposed to be your best man." Luke poured syrup over his pancakes. "Don't have a clue why Molly brought it up."

Clint picked at the ribbon and finally tore it off. The packet contained two heart-shaped cookies decorated with pink icing and silver sprinkles. He broke one in half and stuffed it into his mouth.

Luke laughed at him, then settled into eating his breakfast.

Clint glanced at the newspaper again. It seemed like every merchant in town had some kind of Valentine's Day sale going on. Each ad decorated with red and pink hearts was another reminder of what this week should have been.

"Any regrets?" Luke asked between mouthfuls of his food.

Clint shook his head. "We made the right decision. At least we changed our minds before shelling out too much money for a caterer and a florist."

"Ten years from now, you and I will probably still be sitting in this booth bemoaning our bachelor status during the most romantic week of the year."

"That's probably true." Clint folded up the paper. "But right now, I'd better get to the office. What about you?"

"I'm making the rounds of the thrift stores," Luke answered. "You never know what someone might have dropped off over the weekend."

"Searching for anything in particular?"

"You know me. I won't know till I see it."

Luke was four years younger than Clint. Unlike Clint, whose parents had both been teachers until they retired to Florida, Luke was the heir to a neglected estate west of Magnolia Harbor. Old Man Brannick, Luke's grandfather, lived in an upscale assisted-living facility. The family wasn't destitute—town gossip said that Luke still received money from a trust fund—but there wasn't enough cash to restore Foxsong Meadows to its former glory. Luke didn't even live in the mansion. He claimed that the place was too big and drafty for him. Instead, he'd fixed up the gatehouse for his home. Clint had designed the landscaping.

Luke had gotten a business degree from Clemson University, then decided corporate life wasn't for him. When he returned to Magnolia Harbor, he opened his own business creating sculptures and other artwork from found objects and other people's discards. What some folks called junk.

But Luke had an artistic eye and talent to match. Clint often bought Luke's pieces or commissioned specific ones to use in the gardens he restored for the historic plantations in the state.

It was funny how the differences in age and social status had separated them as children but didn't matter now that they were adults.

The men chatted for a few more moments. Then Clint paid his bill and left.

He drove to Magnolia Harbor and parked. On the walk to his office, he paused outside the Dragonfly Coffee Shop. The window display teemed with hearts, specialty pastries and cookies, and other Valentine-inspired treats.

He hadn't lied to Luke. The sad truth was that he hadn't been nearly as devastated by his broken engagement as he probably should have been. What did that say about him? About his relationship with the woman he'd asked to share the rest of his life? Clint probably wouldn't be giving it that much thought now if she hadn't picked February 14 as their wedding date. How could he get away from the reminders when they were everywhere?

Clint greeted his longtime office manager, Bonnie, as he made his way to his desk. He sifted through the pile of mail she'd placed there earlier. He tossed a few items into his in-box tray and examined the two remaining envelopes. The cream-colored one didn't have a return address, and he didn't recognize the handwriting. It was probably a greeting card.

He smirked. Maybe someone had sent him a Valentine.

Clint slit open the envelope and pulled out the card.

Not a Valentine.

A hundred times worse.

He stared at the wedding card and the generous check from a great-aunt he barely knew. Apparently, she hadn't gotten the news that the wedding had been canceled.

He'd have to call his mom for advice on what to do. But not today. Probably not even this week. Mom had taken the news of the broken engagement pretty hard.

Clint opened the second envelope. The card was a save the date for his ten-year reunion at Harbor High School.

He plopped into his chair and tapped the card against his chin. Ten years already. As if he'd needed the reminder.

At least he could say he'd done fairly well for himself. By working hard, sometimes two or three jobs at a time, he'd managed to pay the difference between the scholarship he'd received and his total school bill. He'd graduated with a degree from the University of South Carolina as a landscape architect after interning each summer with a company in Savannah. A year later, he'd established his own company back home in Magnolia Harbor with the assistance of his mentor.

Creating historic gardens for the renovated estates and plantations in the area combined his primary interests—history and nature. Nothing was more satisfying to his creative spirit than visiting the grounds of an estate he had designed four or six months after completing his work and seeing how his vision had come together with the growth of the plants he'd selected or with a change of seasons.

He tossed the card onto his desk. A decade was too long to hold on to childish dreams. He'd been too young back then to give away his heart so completely. At least that was what he'd repeatedly told himself.

But several years ago, Clint had done what he could in an attempt to get closure. It was a ridiculous thing he hadn't confided to anyone.

After that, his heart had been free enough, open enough, to love again.

Or so he thought.

He'd believed in his love for Margot, but their commitment to each other was tested when she decided to accept a job offer in California and he wanted to stay in Magnolia Harbor. He'd been hurt when they agreed to break off their engagement. And embarrassed. But most of all, he'd been relieved. Something else he'd kept to himself.

They could have been happy together. He was sure of that. But theirs wasn't the love of poems and fairy tales. If so, the breakup wouldn't have been as friendly or as easy.

Clint swiveled his chair to face the long shelves lining one wall and stared at the rusted metal box nestled against a row of old textbooks. It once held pleasant memories and promises of a happy ever after.

But now only heartache could be found inside.

6

Grace

As soon as the guests in the Buttercup and Dogwood Suites checked out on Monday morning, Grace rushed up the stairs with Winston on her heels. The dog supervised as she stripped the beds and cleaned.

When the rooms had been vacuumed, dusted, and polished to her satisfaction, she placed fresh linens on the beds and fluffed the pillows. Justin and Bethany were staying in the Bluebell Suite. They were out, so she refreshed their room, then headed to the third-floor Wisteria Loft Suite.

This suite, on the same floor as the attic, hadn't been used over the weekend. Hopefully, its next occupant, the New York fashion designer, would appreciate its pristine appearance. Especially after Grace added a flower arrangement.

Winston followed Grace to the kitchen.

Charlotte was getting a head start on the hors d'oeuvres for the evening's hospitality hour. Capers fried on the stove while she stirred a mixture of crabmeat and other fresh ingredients. Baskets of strawberries along with bars of dark chocolate sat on the counter. A pot of eggs bubbled on a back burner.

Winston plopped down on the floor with a sigh.

"Someone's exhausted," Charlotte said, then glanced at Grace. "You look beat as well. Were you too busy dreaming of a special someone to get much sleep?"

"Not dreaming exactly." Just a lot of tossing and turning as Grace replayed conversations from the night before. As if she were a college coed instead of a sensible woman in her forties.

"I'm afraid I ruined the mood," Charlotte said.

"I'm not sure there was any mood to ruin." Grace didn't want to talk about last night, so she changed the subject. "Were the flowers delivered?"

Charlotte nodded. "They're in a bucket in the utility room. An assortment of roses. Red, yellow, and white. And lilies of the valley and ferns for filler."

"I'll arrange the vases after lunch." Grace retrieved deli meat and cheese from the fridge along with condiments and a jar of pickles. "Want me to make you a sandwich while I've got all this out?"

"If you don't mind."

Grace opened a loaf of artisan oat nut bread, expecting Charlotte to bombard her with more questions at any moment. When the room remained quiet, Grace turned her gaze from the cracked-pepper turkey and Havarti cheese she was layering onto slices of bread toward her sister.

Charlotte stared at her, self-pity mingling with guilt on her face. "I'm really sorry about last night. I didn't mean to intrude. I was going over the notes that Winnie and I had made for this week's menus when I heard Spencer's car. I couldn't resist peeking out the window. When he saw me, I wanted to crawl into a hole and hide."

"I'm not sure you have anything to feel sorry for. It was late. We were both ready for the evening to end." That might be a little white lie. Grace couldn't speak for Spencer, but she couldn't help wondering how the date—if it was a date—would have ended if Charlotte hadn't been there.

"Did you have a good time?" Charlotte asked.

"A great time." Grace focused on the tomato she was slicing. This one was juicy and red. But it wouldn't have the same luscious flavor of a tomato taken straight from the garden. Or, more accurately, straight from the bin at the local farmers market. "I'm glad to have a friend nearby who enjoys many of the same things that I do."

"A friend, huh?" Charlotte removed the eggs from the stove and rinsed them in cold water. "So . . ."

"No." Grace added the tomato slices to the sandwiches. "It wasn't a date."

"I'm sorry."

"There you go apologizing again, but there's no need," Grace said. She finished the sandwiches and took a seat at the island. "We had fun, and I'm glad we went."

"Did you make any plans for Valentine's Day?" Charlotte asked.

"Maybe we'll go kayaking again," Grace joked.

Charlotte responded with a small laugh, just as Grace had hoped she would.

Grace didn't want to talk about Valentine's Day as it related to her own heart. Her role as hostess of the inn was to make sure her guests had a memorable stay. With most of the rooms occupied, she'd be too busy to think about romance. At least as far as she was concerned.

But perhaps she could help her sister by giving Cupid a hand. An idea had been formulating in her brain since she and Spencer had talked last night about Dean's chef duties at The Tidewater.

"What about you?" she asked. "Do you and Dean have plans?"

"Not really. He'll be working late." Charlotte poured glasses of iced tea and sat down next to Grace. "I'm hoping he'll plan something for Saturday. But so far he hasn't mentioned anything."

"A downside to dating a popular chef."

"It's a small one considering all the upsides," Charlotte replied.

"I'm glad you see it that way." Though Grace wasn't the least bit surprised. Charlotte had once worked as a chef at a popular restaurant in Charleston. She understood the obligations of the profession.

They ate their sandwiches in silence for a few minutes, and then Charlotte said, "We'll just do what we've always done."

"Be each other's valentine?" Grace asked. "Sounds like an excellent idea to me."

The tradition had started long ago—the year after Grace's husband had been killed in a train accident while traveling in Prague on a business trip. Charlotte had been a young teenager, but she couldn't bear the thought of Grace not receiving her usual dozen roses and a box of gourmet chocolates. So Charlotte had saved up her allowance, took on extra babysitting chores, and even sold cookies to her friends at school to make the day special for Grace.

It had been difficult not to fall apart at her little sister's compassionate gift. But Grace had managed to keep her composure while conveying her appreciation. But later when Jake—Grace's son, who had been only a toddler—was asleep, she collapsed into tears on her bed. The next year, she was prepared with a gift for Charlotte.

The pain of grief had eased over the years, and the tradition of being each other's valentine had taken hold. It was a way to stay close—something the sisters needed to work at given the difference in their ages and the seasons of their lives. Grace was married and had a child of her own when Charlotte was only ten. They both loved working together now at the inn. It seemed to make up for all those years when they'd lived apart.

But perhaps Grace could make this Valentine's Day a very special one for her sister and the handsome man she was dating.

If only she could figure out a plan.

7

Presley

As she neared the inn's driveway, Presley resisted the temptation to floor the accelerator on the rental car, a sophisticated dark-blue BMW. Instead, she stared through the windshield, eager for her first glimpse of the restored mansion.

When the inn came into view, she gently pressed the brake and parked on the side of the road. She stepped out, craning her neck to see the three-story antebellum mansion visible through the old, stately trees.

It was her grandparents' house. And yet it wasn't.

Even from this distance, the windows sparkled in the sunshine. The mansion shone with fresh paint, and the roof was bright and solid. The columns appeared sturdier, even bigger. Had they been replaced?

The new owners had definitely put a lot of work and effort into renovating the mansion's exterior. From the photos Presley had seen online, the interior had also undergone a massive transformation. It was almost like going to a place she'd never been before. Except there was a familiarity in the air—perhaps the hint of jasmine on the breeze. Though the fragrance had to be a figment of her imagination. Jasmine didn't grow this time of year.

Despite the winter chill, Presley imagined a summer sun shining upon her. She breathed a prayer of thanks for the familiar sensations flowing through her. Welcoming her back to where she belonged. Where she had longed to be for all these years.

If only she could stay.

But staying was impossible. Coming even for a week was a risk.

Her only consolation was that Clint had no idea she was in town, and she could easily avoid him. Though perhaps it wouldn't matter even if he did know. He might not want to see her after the way she'd hurt him. But there had been no chance for Presley to explain. No chance to make things right. With any luck, his marriage had already taken place and he'd be too happy in his new life to give her a passing thought.

The engagement announcement hadn't listed the date of the wedding, but Presley could have easily found out by doing an Internet search or even browsing the online editions of the local newspapers. But she didn't want to know. The less she knew about Clint in the present, the easier it was to keep him buried in the past.

A black SUV pulled beside her, and the passenger window slid down. The driver leaned across the seat. He appeared to be about her age, with hair a few shades lighter than her own. "Everything okay?" he asked.

"Fine. I was just looking at the house." Presley gestured toward the mansion.

"That's the Magnolia Harbor Inn, isn't it? At least I hope so." The man got out of the vehicle and joined her. "I already missed one turn. Wouldn't think that'd happen with a built-in navigational system, but I always mute the voice. Seems it always has something to say during my favorite songs."

"Like, 'turn here'?" she joked.

His good-natured laugh revealed strong white teeth and drew Presley from her somber mood. "I wasn't in a hurry anyway. You might as well enjoy the trip if you're going to make it."

"That almost sounds like a philosophy for life," Presley remarked.

"Maybe it is."

But not for her. Shiloh had labeled her professional troubles as a pothole. But to Presley, they were a sinkhole. She'd gotten over her anger at Adriana's deception—at least, she hoped she had—but beneath that anger was disappointment at her colleague's betrayal.

As far as this particular trip was concerned, she'd dreaded each passing mile. Why had she even come?

The stranger shoved his hands into his pockets and leaned against the SUV. "So, is this the Magnolia Harbor Inn? Or do I need to unmute the voice on the GPS?"

"You have reached your destination," Presley intoned in a robotic voice.

He laughed again. "Are you from around here?"

"Nope. Just visiting."

"I thought so." His eyes sparkled with humor. "I saw you on the plane. At baggage claim. And at the car rental counter."

"You did?" Presley didn't remember seeing him. But then she'd been too caught up in her own thoughts to pay attention to her fellow passengers.

"Don't worry. I'm not a stalker." He gestured toward the mansion. "I have a reservation there."

She hadn't expected to talk to any of the other guests. Come to think of it, she hadn't even considered other people would be staying at the inn. Which seemed ridiculous considering it was a bed-and-breakfast. "I have a reservation there too."

"Then why are you parked here? If you don't mind my asking."

As Presley considered how to answer, she felt heat rise to her face.

"Forget I asked," he said in an apologetic tone. "Sometimes I talk too much."

"No, it's all right." She regained her composure and held up her phone. "It's so lovely from here that I wanted to take a photo." Fumbling with the screen, she took a couple of shots as if to prove that had been her intention.

"You want me to take one of you with the house in the background?" he offered.

Presley mulled over the question, then smiled. "Why not?" If she didn't like the photo, she could always delete it. But maybe it would be a photo she'd appreciate having years from now. When the intense sadness from being here without her grandparents would no longer grip her heart. "Thanks," she said as she handed him her phone.

As they discussed the best place for her to stand, Presley felt like a model at a photography shoot instead of the designer who stayed behind the scenes. She found herself relaxing for the first time since she decided to make this trip.

After snapping a few photos, he held her phone so they could both see the images.

"You're good at this," she said. "Are you a photographer?"

"No." He grinned at her. "But the camera sure does love you. You're very photogenic."

"I've never thought of myself that way." Not when she encountered gorgeous women every day on the job.

"Maybe you should." He held out his hand. "I'm Trent Jacobs."

The name seemed slightly familiar, but she didn't know why. "It's nice to meet you. I'm Presley Ingram."

"Presley? Your parents a fan of the King?"

"My dad was," she replied.

"Was?"

"He left my mom when I was young." *And me.* As if naming her had been his only responsibility.

"I'm sorry."

"Me too." Presley made her voice as light as possible. Her family history wasn't something she usually brought up only minutes after meeting someone. Perhaps she was more tired than she realized. No surprise, since she'd hardly slept last night.

"You're from New York?" Trent asked.

"Yes. I'm a fashion designer."

"See? I knew you had experience in front of the cameras."

She laughed. "Not really. I only design the clothes the models wear. What about you?"

"Also from the Big Apple," he said. "I play football."

"Of course! That's why I know your name."

"Are you a Giants fan?" Trent asked.

"Not really," Presley admitted.

"That's okay. I don't know the first thing about fashion, so I guess we're even," he said. "My sisters insist on taking me shopping at least twice a year so I won't embarrass the family with my lack of style."

Presley made a show of looking him over with a discerning eye. Trent was very handsome in a suede jacket and jeans that were tailored to fit his athletic body perfectly. "Your sisters have excellent taste."

"I'll tell them a professional fashionista complimented them. They'll love it."

"How many sisters do you have?" she asked.

"Four. All younger than me and each a handful."

Presley couldn't help but laugh. "I'm an only child. But I used to pray for a sibling."

"There are days when I'm sure mine would give me away," Trent said, smiling.

She returned his easy smile, then glanced toward the inn. Walking through those front doors didn't seem as foreboding now as before. "I suppose we should check in."

"I'll follow you if that's okay."

"In other words, you want me to be your GPS," Presley teased.

"And in return, I'll be your big brother." Trent opened her car door. "Whenever you want one."

"It's a deal." Presley slid into her car.

Trent shut the door before going to his own.

Her earlier unease had disappeared. The laughter she'd experienced with Trent seemed to have reawakened the warmth and excitement she'd always felt when arriving at her grandparents' home. When she was a child, the house hadn't been ramshackle but a delightful place with secret nooks and crannies waiting to be explored.

Waiting for her and Clint.

She shook her head. This trip wasn't about Clint.

Okay, it was. But only Clint from the past. Not Clint from now. She'd do what she came to do and leave.

Clint would never even know she'd been here.

Presley followed Trent into the inn. When she glanced around, she almost gasped. The foyer featured a gleaming marble floor, an elaborate chandelier, and a sweeping staircase. It was magnificent. She could hardly believe it used to be her grandparents' home.

A dark-haired woman smiled at them from behind the front desk. "Welcome to the Magnolia Harbor Inn. I'm Grace Porter, one of the owners. You must be Presley Ingram and Trent Jacobs."

Presley nodded. "Your inn is beautiful."

"Thank you," Grace said. "I hope you both enjoy your stay."

A blonde woman and a tall dark-haired man walked into the room with a little brown dog trotting behind them.

Grace turned to the couple. "You're just in time to meet Presley and Trent."

The blonde woman smiled. "I'm Charlotte Wylde, Grace's sister, and this is Dean Bradley, the owner and chef of The Tidewater across the lake."

The dog yipped, making everyone laugh.

"And we can't forget Winston," Grace said.

"What an honor to meet you," Dean said to Trent. "What brings you to town?"

"I'm here for a business meeting," Trent answered but didn't elaborate.

"Please let me check in my guests before you mob them," Grace told Dean with a laugh.

After they filled out the paperwork, the sisters offered to show Presley and Trent to their rooms. Charlotte took Trent to the second floor, and Grace accompanied Presley to the Wisteria Loft Suite on the third floor.

Presley stared in awe when Grace opened the door to the room. A large steamer trunk sat at the foot of a regal king-size bed covered with a blue comforter, creamy linens, and an assortment of pillows. Antique chairs flanked the substantial fireplace, and a vase of beautifully arranged yellow roses, delicate white lilies of the valley, and deep green ferns adorned a cherry table. French doors, outlined with blue drapes, permitted a rectangle of sunlight to reflect the polished wood floor and highlight the pattern of the tapestry rug that anchored the bed and trunk.

The suite was breathtakingly gorgeous. It seemed that every wall, every floorboard, every corner had been transformed. Presley had studied the online photos of the suite, so she had expected the change. But seeing the room in person wasn't the same, and she struggled to accept that this was where she had spent almost all her childhood summers.

"Is something wrong?" Grace's concerned voice broke through Presley's trance. "This is the suite you requested, but if it doesn't suit . . . Well, I can move you to the Rosebud Suite if you don't mind sharing a bathroom."

"It's lovely," Presley said. "Lovelier than I ever imagined."

"I'm so glad you like it," Grace responded. "It's not our most popular suite because of all the stairs. But I think it's always been my favorite."

Presley set her bag on the luggage rack and somehow managed a nonchalant tone despite the nerves assailing her stomach. "Why is that?"

"I don't know if I can give you a reason. At least not without sounding fanciful. Or maybe even a little crazy."

Her curiosity piqued, Presley wandered toward the fireplace as if to study the landscape hanging above the mantel. "Tell me."

"Like most of the other rooms, it needed a complete renovation. But it had a different feel to it. As if it were a happy room with echoes of dreams and hopes." Grace gave a deprecating smile, and her cheeks flushed. "I told you it sounded crazy."

"I don't think so." Presley gazed at the beam of sunlight shining through the French doors. How often had she sat on her bed—not a bed as luxurious as this but still a comfortable one—and sketched on her pad between long glances through the tall windows the doors had replaced? She'd had all kinds of hopes and dreams. Most of them involved fame and riches so she could shower her grandparents with money. Then they could have restored their own home instead of giving these strangers the privilege.

Presley was a household name only in the fashion world, and over time she had amassed a healthy bank account. Though her innovative designs brought her early success, the money hadn't come soon enough to make her dream come true. Now all she had left were memories.

She turned to Grace. "It seems to me that a house as old as this one must be affected by the people who lived here."

"I agree." Grace regarded the room as if seeing it with new eyes. "My sister and I knew the moment we saw this mansion that it was the perfect place for us. We've done everything we could to keep as much of the original woodwork as possible. Other features too."

"Like the fireplace," Presley said softly. "I mean, I assume there was a fireplace here before you renovated," she hurriedly added. She didn't want to say anything, no matter how unintentional, that would lead Grace to suspect she'd been here before.

"Yes, it's the original." Grace placed the key on a side table. "I'll leave you to get settled. We have a hospitality hour from six to seven. I hope you'll join us on the back veranda. If it's too cold, it'll be in the dining room. And if you need anything, please let me know."

"Thank you." Presley rubbed her forearms, feeling a sudden chill. "I'll be there."

After Grace left, Presley knelt in front of the fireplace to examine the interior. The bricks had been cleaned and painted white, but she didn't think they'd been replaced. If the outer bricks were the original, the interior bricks probably were too.

She pushed up her sleeve and reached inside the chimney. Her fingers touched the jagged corner of a cracked brick. From that starting point, she walked her fingers downward. One brick. Two bricks. Three bricks. Then to the right. One. Two.

Presley gripped the edges and tugged. The brick barely moved. She tried again, gaining better purchase, and wiggled the brick from side to side. Eventually it gave way. She took a deep breath and hoped she wouldn't touch a spiderweb or a decaying insect. Then she reached inside the crevice and pulled out a package wrapped in a canvas bag.

With a sigh of satisfaction, Presley carried the package through the French doors and out onto the veranda. A cool breeze loosened a few strands of her hair, and she involuntarily shivered. Despite the chill, she lowered herself to the plank floor, her back against the exterior wall of the house, and brushed away the dirt and dust from the bag.

Faraway laughter floated up on the breeze, and Presley turned her attention from the package to the expansive lawn. Charlotte and Dean walked hand in hand across the lawn toward the old chapel. But it wasn't the old chapel anymore. Apparently, the sisters' renovations had also included the dilapidated structure. It appeared bright and fresh too.

When Presley and Trent had arrived, Dean had seemed impressed to meet the famous athlete. Presley was surprised Charlotte had managed to tear him away from the football star.

Like she couldn't tear her eyes away from watching the couple as they strolled across the lawn. Dean bent toward Charlotte as if he didn't want to miss a word she was saying. The intimate gesture, so simple yet so romantic, tore at Presley's heart.

Why couldn't that have been Clint and me?

She brought up her legs and pressed the package between her knees and her forehead. The tears she had held back for days flowed down her cheeks.

It was too late to change the past. Grandma used to say it was set in concrete.

But hopefully it wasn't too late to reclaim one small piece of it.

8

Grace

Roger and Joy Phillips arrived about half an hour after Presley and Trent. Grace got the honeymooning couple settled into their suite, then called Charlotte to let her know she had books to return to the library.

When that errand was done, Grace parked in a public lot. It was time to take care of the real reason she'd come to town. She walked to Spool & Thread.

Judith Mason, the owner of the fabric shop, along with Winnie and Helen Daley were gathered around a long table. They were three of the five members of The Busy Bees quilting group.

"Hope I'm not intruding," Grace said. "Is this a formal meeting?"

Judith beamed at her. "Not at all."

"We're putting the finishing touches on the preemie quilts." Winnie held up a decorative cardboard heart attached to a silver ribbon. "A special tag goes on each one to let the family know the quilt was made with love and prayer."

"That's such a wonderful ministry." Grace ran her fingers lightly over the nearest quilt, a simple nine patch made from star-themed cotton fabric. The border was a sumptuous blue with tiny white dots.

The Busy Bees donated several cotton and flannel quilts each year to the local Northshore Medical Center as well as a hospital in Charleston that specialized in high-risk pregnancy and neonatal care.

"I'm sure these quilts become precious keepsakes," Grace continued.

"I hope you're right," Winnie said as she pinned the tag to one of the quilts.

"You're welcome to join us anytime," Helen told Grace. She massaged her index finger with her thumb. "My arthritis has been flaring up more than usual the past few weeks. I may not be able to make many more of these quilts."

"Thank you," Grace said. "There's always so much to do at the inn, and it's difficult to get away."

"Just know there's always a place for you here when you need it," Helen said.

"And for you, Helen," Judith chimed in. "Whether you're here to make quilts or join in the conversation. The Busy Bees wouldn't be the same without you."

"I certainly don't plan on missing any meetings," Helen said. "Tuesday nights wouldn't be the same without getting together with my peeps." She chuckled. "Isn't that what the young folks say these days?"

The women laughed, then chatted about their grandchildren's strange expressions. That led to laughter over their own odd sayings that had caused their parents to roll their eyes.

When the conversation died down, Winnie turned to Grace who'd taken a chair opposite her. "What brings you to town this time of day? Have all the guests arrived?"

"They're all here," Grace answered. "I wanted to talk to you in private."

"Why didn't you say so?" Winnie started to stand.

Grace reached across the table to stop her. "No, I meant in private from Charlotte." She smiled at the other women. "Maybe you all could help too."

"We surely will if we can," Judith said as she lined boxes with pink and blue tissue paper. "Is Charlotte up to some kind of mischief?"

"No, nothing like that," Grace answered. "It's about Valentine's Day."

The women put down their work and gave her their full attention.

"It's hard for Dean to get away from the restaurant on such a special day," Grace said. "After all, he's the chef. He has to be there to make sure the diners are satisfied."

"Which means he can't take Charlotte out for a romantic dinner of their own," Winnie said. "Do you think they'll make plans for Saturday? Or maybe Thursday?"

"They might," Grace replied. "But I'd like to do something special for them *on* Valentine's Day. Even though it's hectic and they'll both be busy. I just don't know what. I thought you might have an idea."

"This sounds like a perfect project for The Busy Bees," Judith said. "We'll come up with something they'll never forget."

"Thank you all so much," Grace said.

Someone's phone dinged, and Winnie pulled hers from a pocket. She read the screen with a slight frown, then tapped on it.

"Anything wrong?" Grace asked.

"Nothing to bother you with." Winnie handed Grace a stack of the heart tags and a spool of ribbon. "But I do need to run. Could you finish putting the tags together and pinning them onto the quilts for me?"

Grace readily agreed, but she studied her aunt with concern. "Are you sure everything is okay? Was that Charlotte?"

"Everything is fine. I'm simply needed elsewhere." Winnie gathered her belongings and kissed Grace on the top of her head as she came behind her chair. "I'll see you all tomorrow evening," she said with a wave.

"That was strange," Grace remarked after Winnie left.

"Don't let it worry you," Judith said. "Your aunt is a busy lady. A lot of people count on her wisdom and advice."

"That's true," Helen said. "None of us could ask for a better friend or neighbor."

"Or a more discreet one." Judith meticulously folded one of the tiny quilts to fit inside a box. "I imagine she knows more of the goings-on in Magnolia Harbor than the rest of us combined."

Grace smiled politely and refrained from responding. Judith was the one with an inside scoop on the town's gossip. Though, like Winnie, Judith never told anything she shouldn't, which made them popular confidants.

If Winnie wanted Grace to know where she was going, she would have told her. Maybe she would explain later. Grace inwardly smiled at her own curiosity while she threaded strands of ribbon through the heart tags and pinned them to the quilts.

At least now she had allies in her quest to make this a memorable Valentine's Day for Charlotte and Dean.

That in itself would make it a memorable Valentine's Day for her too, even though she didn't have a valentine to call her own.

9

Winnie

The cottage door opened before Winnie reached it.

Charlotte glanced around before pulling her aunt inside. "Did anyone see you?" she whispered.

"I don't think so." As Winnie placed her bag on a nearby table, a noise from the kitchen startled her. The cottage was basically one long room with jutting beams that defined each space. But Winnie's attention had been on Charlotte, and she hadn't realized anyone was skulking in the kitchen.

Spencer greeted Winnie with a smile. "The kettle just boiled. Would you like a cup of tea?"

"I think I would," Winnie answered. She followed Charlotte to the round oak table in the kitchen and took a seat, all the while speculating on the reason for her summons. The text she'd received at Spool & Thread had been from her younger niece. Charlotte didn't know Grace was with Winnie at the time, but her message said she needed to see Winnie without Grace's knowledge. Hopefully, Grace would be at the fabric store working on the task Winnie had given her for a little while longer.

"I'm so glad you came." Charlotte placed a tray of snacks on the table, then sat down. "We need your help. Or, to be more precise, Spencer needs our help."

"What's wrong?" Winnie asked him.

Spencer poured hot tea into china cups. "Nothing's really wrong." He returned the kettle to the stove and joined them at the table. His fingers twitched as he gripped a napkin. "I only wanted to see if I could get your advice about something."

Winnie sipped her tea to hide a smile. The retired FBI intelligence analyst, usually so composed, was rarely nervous.

"I came to ask Charlotte for help," Spencer continued. He leaned forward. "I want to do something special for Grace on Valentine's Day. But I know she might be busy with her guests during the day. Dean said he'd try to squeeze us in at The Tidewater, but neither of us likes a crowd."

Winnie touched his arm. "Have you asked Grace what she'd like to do?"

"No, I haven't," Spencer said. "I was hoping to surprise her, but I'm not sure how to do it."

Winnie took another sip of her tea. The Busy Bees had already promised to help Grace come up with a Valentine's Day plan for Charlotte and Dean. The group might as well do the same for Charlotte and Spencer and plan a Valentine's Day surprise for Grace too.

"Leave it to me," Winnie said with a smile. "I'll ask The Busy Bees. I'm sure we can come up with something."

The obvious relief on Spencer's face warmed Winnie's heart. The man looked like an enormous weight had been lifted from his shoulders. "Thank you. Just tell me what you need me to do. And don't worry about the expense."

"Don't do anything yet," Winnie told him. She thought for a moment and faced Charlotte. "But maybe you should make plans with Grace for that evening. Then she won't suspect anything." *And neither will you.* Perhaps that would make it easier to keep them in the dark about any plans The Busy Bees came up with. At least Winnie hoped so.

"Leave it to me," Charlotte said. "We've been each other's valentines for a while now, so she won't think it's strange. In fact, we've already talked about it."

"That's good," Winnie said.

Charlotte gripped Spencer's arm. "I'm thrilled for you and Grace. It will be so much fun, and I know it'll make her happy." Her enthusiasm seemed to dim. "Dean has to spend the evening at The Tidewater, so we can't really celebrate. At least not on Valentine's Day."

"Have you made plans for another day?" Winnie asked as innocently as she could.

"Not really," Charlotte answered. "I thought he was going to talk to me about it earlier today, but then he got so excited about meeting Trent Jacobs. Apparently, any thought of romance or dating went right out of his head."

"The football player?" Spencer asked. "I'd like to meet him."

"Not you too," Charlotte teased. "We also have an award-winning New York fashion designer as a guest. Will you swoon over her?"

"I'm not swooning," Spencer said. "But this is Trent Jacobs we're talking about."

"You can join us for the hospitality hour if you'd like, but I can't guarantee he'll be there." Charlotte checked the clock. "Speaking of which, I'd better get over to the kitchen. Winnie, let me know what you need me to do for Spencer's surprise. I could plan the menu."

"I appreciate the offer." Winnie finished her tea. "Time for me to go home and see what my own valentine wants to do for supper tonight."

"You know," Charlotte said, "Trent and Presley would make an attractive couple. Maybe we could give them a nudge in the romance department too."

"Who's Presley?" Spencer asked.

"The fashion designer."

He grabbed a cookie. "How do you know they don't already have significant others?"

"They might," Charlotte said. "But I don't think so."

"Why not?" Spencer asked.

"For a former agent, you're not very astute in matters of the heart," Winnie teased.

He cocked his head. "What am I missing?"

"Perhaps an important bit of information," Winnie said. "They're both staying through the weekend."

"Ah," Spencer said knowingly. "If they already had significant others in their lives, they wouldn't be doing that."

"No, I don't think they would." Winnie turned to Charlotte. "But I plan to keep my Cupid arrows directed only at Grace." *And you and Dean.* "I suggest you do the same."

"I'm not making any promises," Charlotte said. "We're having romantic snacks and treats all week. Who knows what effect they'll have on our unattached guests?"

Spencer chuckled. "If Trent and Presley end up married because of your culinary creations, you could write a new cookbook. Call it *Cupid's Creations.* I'm sure it would outsell everything else out there."

"I can see it now," Charlotte said. "All hearts and flowers and chocolate."

"If anyone can do it, you can," Winnie said as she retrieved her bag and pulled out her car key. "I'll be in touch with both of you soon."

"Thanks, Winnie." Spencer walked with her and Charlotte to the door. "This really does mean a lot to me."

"Grace means a lot to me," Winnie said. "And you're a good man." Just the man Grace needed in her life. Maybe by this time next year . . . but no. It was too soon to make *those* kinds of plans.

Her focus needed to be on Valentine's Day.

And juggling two secret romantic dates.

10

Grace

The weather was a little cool as the sun rested on the distant horizon. Grace and Charlotte had debated whether to move their hospitality hour indoors, but the guests had dressed for the chill and seemed to be enjoying the hors d'oeuvres, treats, hot chocolate, and wine that the women had set out on a long buffet table.

Charlotte's crab puffs were baked to golden-brown perfection. The deviled eggs, garnished with chives and bits of red pepper, were the ideal accompaniment. The strawberries had been dipped in melted dark chocolate and frozen.

Justin, Bethany, Roger, and Joy sat together at a table while Presley and Trent settled next to each other in the cushioned rocking chairs.

Grace stopped next to the table. "Did you all enjoy your day?"

"We had a great time." Bethany nudged her husband. "Didn't we?"

"We went on a walking tour of Charleston." Justin gave her a teasing smile. "Now I can cross that off my bucket list."

"We're doing that later this week," Joy said. "Did you really enjoy it?"

"Absolutely," Bethany answered. "The houses are so beautiful, and I loved hearing about their history."

"We're going sailing on Wednesday." Justin dipped a crab puff into Charlotte's tangy sweet-and-sour sauce. "That's what I'm excited about."

"Now that sounds like a bucket list item." Roger squeezed Joy's hand. "Think we could fit something like that into the itinerary?"

"As long as we can visit a few antique stores while we're here."

Joy and her husband shared a lingering gaze. "I'm fine with whatever you want to do."

Grace smiled. Romance definitely was in the air. "If any of you need help with planning or recommendations, let me know. We want you to have a memorable time while you're with us."

"What's the best seafood restaurant along the coast?" Justin asked.

Grace named a couple of her favorites, then excused herself and joined Charlotte at the other end of the porch.

Charlotte wrapped her arms around herself and whispered, "I'm confused. Which ones are the newlyweds?"

Grace couldn't help but grin. She'd also been surprised when the newlyweds arrived. "Roger and Joy. The older ones."

"They're old enough to be Justin and Bethany's parents," Charlotte said. "I was expecting newlyweds. I mean, young newlyweds."

"To be honest, so was I." Grace glanced over at the table where the two couples appeared to be having a good time together. Joy shivered, and Roger placed his arm around her shoulders. "It's a second marriage for both of them. But they're just as starry-eyed as any of the young honeymooning couples we've had staying with us."

Charlotte smiled. "It's adorable."

"Yes, it is." Grace averted her gaze when Joy leaned into her husband's warmth. A pang of grief, sharper than she'd felt in a long time, squeezed her heart. She'd known moments like that once, but not nearly enough of them. She'd been only twenty-six when she'd received the call that Hank had died.

Two of Hank's colleagues had died in the same accident, and for a while, Grace and the other spouses had supported one another. But long years had passed, and they'd drifted apart. One who'd been slightly older than Grace with two young children had remarried years ago. She'd had two more children since then. Each year, she sent a Christmas card photo of the family. It was about the only contact they had with each other anymore.

Charlotte released a small sigh. "They seem so happy."

Winston trotted over to Grace and whined.

Grace smiled at the sweet dog. He seemed to sense when she needed to be cheered up. As she scratched behind Winston's ears, she pushed away the thoughts that could easily lead her into gloom. Then she focused on their guests. "Those two seem to be enjoying each other's company." She nodded toward Presley and Trent.

"No surprise," Charlotte said. "They're about the same age. Both from New York and successful in their fields. I suppose they have a lot in common."

As if he'd sensed they were talking about him, Trent rose and came toward them. Presley followed him.

"Are you having a nice evening?" Grace asked. She gestured to the buffet table. "We have plenty of food left."

"I'll have to go on a diet when I get home," Trent said, patting his stomach. "Or my coach will assign me extra time in the weight room."

Grace laughed. The young athlete didn't look like he had an ounce of fat on his body.

"Speaking of food," Trent said. "Could you recommend somewhere we can go for a late supper?"

"Nothing fancy," Presley added. "I'm not interested in spending extra time in the weight room either. Though if you feed us like this every evening, I won't have a choice. The crab puffs were especially tasty."

"I'm glad you enjoyed them," Charlotte said. "I never make them exactly the same way twice, but I'd be glad to give you a basic recipe if you'd like."

Presley laughed. "That's kind of you, but I don't get the opportunity to cook very often. It's easier to eat out or order in."

"Life in New York," Charlotte breathed. "It sounds so exciting."

"I'll take that recipe if you don't mind," Trent said. "When my team isn't playing in the Super Bowl, I drown my sorrows by throwing a huge party. We spend all day in the kitchen. Mom and my sisters cooking and stirring and baking. Dad and me tasting and supervising."

"I'll bet they love you for that," Charlotte said with a smile. "I'll jot down the recipe for you."

"Well, that was what you might call a bit of an exaggeration," Trent admitted. "When we were growing up, meals were a family affair, and Mom made sure we all knew our way around the kitchen. Even me. I can't make you a five-star gourmet meal, but you'll never leave my table hungry."

Grace decided that Trent was a fine man. Confident but not arrogant. Successful but not egotistical. She imagined his family kept him grounded.

While he and Charlotte talked about party appetizers, Grace glanced at Presley. Her fingers cradled a deviled egg as if she'd forgotten she had picked it up. She stared toward the lake, and she seemed a million miles away.

Grace followed her gaze but couldn't figure out what held Presley's attention. The slanting sunlight on the waves was breathtaking. But Grace sensed something more than a spectacular sunset held the woman in its grasp.

At that moment, Presley looked straight at Grace, and her large brown eyes held incredible sadness. She startled, blinked, then stared at her plate.

Grace touched Presley's arm. When she met her guest's eyes, the sadness was gone. Or had Grace imagined it? "Are you all right?" she asked quietly.

"I'm fine," Presley answered. She set her plate on the table next to her empty mug. "I'm not sure why I took all this food. I really can't eat another bite since Trent and I are going out later."

At the mention of his name, Trent turned to Grace and Presley. He smiled at Presley and placed his hand on the small of her back.

Presley returned his smile.

Grace thought that Charlotte was right. They did make an attractive couple.

"Oh yes. You wanted a restaurant recommendation," Charlotte said, breaking into Grace's musings. She nudged her sister. "Where should we send them?"

"How about Aunt Patsy's Porch? They have the best pie—apart from Charlotte's, of course—in a hundred miles," Grace said. "And Southern-style home cooking is their specialty."

"I'll bet you don't get much of that in the city," Charlotte added.

"There are some restaurants that are good, but nothing tastes like the real thing," Presley said.

"Are you originally from the South?" Grace asked in surprise. "I don't hear an accent."

"No, I'm not." Presley sounded as if she regretted that she wasn't. "But I've traveled in this region before."

"Are any of your designs inspired by our Southern charm?" Charlotte asked.

"If you ladies plan on talking about fashion, then maybe you won't mind me leaving you to it. I have a few calls to make." Trevor faced Presley. "How about I meet you in the lobby around eight?"

"I'd like that," Presley said.

"Could you hang around a little while longer?" Charlotte asked Trent. "One of our neighbors hoped to meet you. I thought Spencer would be here by now."

Grace glanced at her sister. "When did you see Spencer?"

"Earlier today. He's a big fan of Trent's." Charlotte's gaze darted toward the lawn, then to the chocolate-dipped strawberries. "I think I'll take these over to our other guests and make sure they don't need anything else." She picked up the tray and hurried to the table where the two couples were chatting.

"Who's Spencer?" Trent asked.

"Like Charlotte said, a neighbor." Grace's cheeks warmed, and she hoped she wasn't visibly blushing. "And a friend."

"Maybe another time then. I really should make these calls." He lightly touched Presley's elbow. "See you later."

Presley nodded.

"Trent seems very nice," Grace commented after he was gone.

"He does, doesn't he?"

"Have you known each other long?" Why had Grace asked that? It was none of her business. "I'm sorry. I didn't mean to pry."

"That's okay. We met when we got here." Presley picked up her mug. "Do you have any more hot chocolate? It has a warm note to it that I can't quite put my finger on. Could it be cayenne?"

"It is cayenne," Charlotte said in delight. She'd returned just in time to hear Presley's comment. "You're definitely a foodie to have picked up on that."

Presley gave a deprecating laugh. "Not a foodie. Just a hot chocolate aficionado."

"I love that," Charlotte said. "I've thought about experimenting with a few different ingredients. How would you like to give me a hand with it sometime during your stay? If you're not too busy, that is."

"I'm not too busy at all," Presley said. "In fact, that sounds fun."

Grace refilled Presley's mug. "Enjoy," she said.

"Thank you." Presley wrapped her hands around the mug and took a sip.

Grace sensed their guest wanted to say something, perhaps ask something, but she wasn't sure how. Or maybe Grace needed to rein in her imagination.

"Would you like to sit and chat for a while?" Grace gestured toward the rockers where Presley and Trent had been sitting. "It's such a lovely evening despite the chill."

Presley stared at the mug as if trying to make up her mind. "That sounds nice."

The women sat down, and Winston curled up at Grace's feet.

"I've always been fascinated by small towns," Presley remarked. "You know, the kind of place where everyone knows everyone else. That kind of thing."

"Magnolia Harbor is like that," Grace said. "Perhaps not as much as it was ten or fifteen years ago. But it still has that small-town charm. I wouldn't want to live anywhere else."

"So you grew up here?" Presley asked, then took a sip of her hot chocolate.

Grace nodded. "Born and raised. Though I went to Clemson for college, then moved to Charleston. I came back when Charlotte and I bought the inn."

"Was it an inn before you bought it?" Presley's voice seemed to waver.

"No, it was someone's home," Grace said. "A lovely mansion—at least it had been at one time. Like many of these old places, there wasn't enough money for the upkeep. But I believe the family who lived here was happy."

"Why do you say that?"

"The house is happy," Grace said. "The first time I walked through the front doors, I felt as if this was meant to be my home. That it was waiting for me to arrive. I don't think a sad or gloomy place would have been as welcoming."

"I suppose not," Presley murmured, then rested her cup, still more than half full, on her knees. "I should go freshen up before meeting Trent."

"It's nice that the two of you are here at the same time," Grace remarked.

"We discovered we know a couple of the same people. Strange, isn't it? In a city as big as New York."

"I doubt it's a coincidence."

"You don't believe in coincidences?" Presley asked.

"Nor chance," Grace said. "God has a purpose for everything."

Presley smiled. "If you think God's purpose was for Trent and me . . . I wouldn't be so sure about that."

"I'm sorry," Grace said lightly. "I suppose romance is in the air with Valentine's Day coming so soon. We can't help but play matchmakers, and, well, you are going out with him this evening."

"Only as friends." Presley smiled again. "But thank you for believing it could have been a possibility." She lowered her voice. "He is quite handsome, isn't he?"

"Yes," Grace said, laughing. "He certainly is. But I imagine you're quite the catch yourself."

"I haven't had much time to think about settling down," Presley admitted. "I've been too focused on my career." Her eyes clouded over, and her voice dropped. "Maybe too focused."

"That can easily happen," Grace said. She could tell that something was bothering Presley, and she wanted to be encouraging without prying into her personal life. Trent had mentioned when he checked in that he was in town for a business meeting. But Presley didn't seem to be here for any particular reason. Maybe she simply needed a restful vacation. If so, she'd come to the right place. The Magnolia Harbor Inn was the perfect spot to rest one's body and soul.

"I used to be in marketing before I opened the inn with my sister," Grace continued, her tone soft and soothing. "That may not be quite as creative a field as fashion design, but I understand the pressure to come up with new campaigns and unique ideas."

"It's a challenge." Presley appeared to withdraw into herself. A moment later, she stirred and turned to Grace. "I suppose marketing is a very competitive field too."

"Definitely. And don't even get me started on the horrors of office politics and overzealous coworkers." Grace had been vice president of new business development at Maddox Creative. She'd had a few rough patches with highly ambitious associates who'd cut ethical corners in their quest to climb the corporate ladder. "I guess that's common in most industries."

"Yes," Presley said. The simple word weighed heavy in the night air.

Grace resisted the urge to speak, allowing space for Presley to talk or remain silent. Out near the lake, the croaking frogs added their own ambience to the peaceful evening.

"Another designer asked me to collaborate with her on a project," Presley said quietly. "I thought we were friends, but she presented all my designs as her own. By the time I found out, she'd already met with the client."

"I'm sorry that happened." Grace rested a comforting hand on Presley's arm. "I suppose you don't have any proof the designs are yours?"

"None. They aren't my usual style." Presley huffed. "I've been in a bit of a slump lately, and I was excited to try something different. I still can't believe she betrayed me."

"I know it hurts," Grace said. "But she's hurt herself too, whether she realizes it yet or not. In my experience, the truth tends to come out eventually."

"The thing is, she's really talented. She doesn't need to cheat." Presley gazed into her mug. "I'm not sure I want to design anymore. At least, not in that kind of environment."

"Maybe it's time for a change," Grace suggested.

"A change to what?" Presley asked. "My whole life revolves around fashion. I don't know if I can leave that world behind. And I'm not sure if I can stay either."

"I can't give you the answer to that question," Grace said. "But I can pray you find it."

Presley's eyes widened. "You'd pray for me?"

"Absolutely."

"My grandparents were praying people," Presley said. "I want to be more like them, but sometimes it can be hard."

The regret in Presley's tone caused Grace's heart to ache for the younger woman. According to what Charlotte had found online about her, she was an extremely talented designer. Yet here she sat, her hands cupped around a mug of hot chocolate, obviously hurt and miserable.

"Praying is easy," Grace encouraged. "God always listens."

Presley smiled at Grace. "You're a good listener too."

"I'm here anytime you want to talk."

A heavy step sounded on the wooden planks, and Trent loomed over them. "I didn't mean to interrupt."

"You didn't," Presley said.

"I'm finished with my calls," he told her. "If you're ready, we could head out to Aunt Patsy's Porch."

"I need to get my bag." Presley scooted to the edge of the rocking chair. "Thank you, Grace. It's been nice talking with you."

"Anytime," Grace said. "It's been nice for me too."

Presley stood and picked up her mug. "I'll be back down in five minutes. Maybe ten."

"Take your time," Trent said. "I'll be waiting."

Presley deposited the mug on a table and left the veranda.

Trent sat down on the rocker Presley had vacated and gave a contented sigh. "This is the life. I wouldn't mind doing this every evening."

"We enjoy it here," Grace said. "Though it has its own unique challenges."

"If things work out the way I hope, you might be seeing more of me."

"Why is that?" she asked.

"There's an opportunity here," he answered. "A fulfillment of a dream, you might say. But my partners and I need to keep it under wraps for now."

Grace's shoulders stiffened as she wondered what kind of opportunity he was talking about. "As long as it's not a big-box store or a giant mall," she said as lightly as possible.

Trent's pleasant laugh floated between them. "Nothing like that, I promise you. What we have in mind is a great fit for this area."

Grace wasn't sure how to respond. The town had dealt with investment schemes before—ones designed to line the developers' pockets while upending the community's appeal as a small-town tourist destination. But the chamber of commerce and town council had always managed to stop anything that would do more harm than good to the local economy and the quality of life the citizens enjoyed here. Whatever Trent and his partners had in mind, she hoped it wasn't one of those kinds of schemes.

Until she knew more, she shouldn't make any unfair judgments. She liked to believe the best of her guests.

11

Presley

The next morning, Presley joined the other guests in the brightly lit dining room. Grace and Charlotte bustled back and forth from the kitchen, serving a delicious breakfast of a thick frittata bubbling with goat cheese and laced with caramelized onions, a selection of muffins and pastries, and fresh fruit.

The dining room, like all the others in the mansion, was beautifully decorated. But Presley missed the large paddle fans that used to cool the room on hot summer days. The fans had been replaced by an ornate chandelier centered over a mahogany table. Decorative shades covered the bulbs, lending to the warmth and elegance of the room.

After breakfast, Presley wandered over to the fireplace. Recessed lighting illuminated a large landscape, framed in gold, that hung over the mantel. A lump caught in Presley's throat. A family portrait once held this place of honor. Grandpa had commissioned a local artist to paint Presley's grandmother and mother to celebrate his only child's tenth birthday.

During her summers here, Presley had often studied the painting, searching for any similarity she had to Mother and finding none. Instead, the curves of her grandmother's cheeks and her angular jaw had skipped a generation. Presley had always found comfort in her resemblance to her grandmother. Perhaps, she'd reasoned, that meant she was more like her grandmother than Mother in other ways too. The ways that mattered.

But she couldn't help wondering if her mother would have loved her more if she'd favored her.

Presley lowered her eyes and turned from the fireplace. What had happened to the portrait? Surely Mother hadn't allowed the estate company to sell it. Or had her resentment of the mansion and her parents overcome any sentiment she might have once felt for the painting?

A swath of sunlight brightened the room, as if a cloud no longer hid the sun, and Presley stepped toward the veranda. One thing hadn't changed. The view of the lake through the French doors still took her breath away. Why couldn't Mother love this place as much as Presley did? If she had, their lives would have been so different.

And their relationship would be so much better.

Presley might be living here instead of paying for the privilege of visiting.

She pushed away the negative thought. Bitterness wouldn't change the past, and she refused to indulge in that poison.

Whatever things are pure, whatever things are lovely ... meditate on these things. The phrase from Philippians 4:8, one she thought she'd forgotten, whispered in her heart and eased the choking lump in her throat.

As she went upstairs to her room, she reminded herself that she needed to focus on why she'd come. Not on the circumstances that had taken her away.

She hadn't summoned the courage to explore the gardens around the mansion after checking in yesterday. But neither could she explain to herself why she needed courage to explore her favorite summertime places. After all, that was why she'd made the trip.

But yesterday's flight after a restless night's sleep had drained her. Add to that the emotions dredged up by seeing the restored mansion for the first time in almost ten years—she couldn't bear to face the changes that surely had been made to the grounds too. Even if Grace and Charlotte had only spruced up the old gardens and flower beds, they'd be different. A lot could change in that amount of time.

So she'd contented herself with lounging on the comfy king-size bed, surrounded by luxurious pillows, as she relived the long summer days she'd spent in the room now known as the Wisteria Loft Suite.

Eventually, she'd unwrapped the package that she'd retrieved from inside the chimney. The scrapbook's cover, decorated with swirls and glitter and pictures cut out from magazines, appeared worn and faded. Just as it had the last time she'd seen it. By then, she'd been adding sketches, photos, movie ticket stubs, and other memorabilia for at least six years. She'd meant to redo the cover that last summer. But somehow she'd never gotten around to it.

Memories had flooded back as she flipped through the pages. Most of the ticket stubs were for matinees that she and Clint had attended at the movie theater. Afterward, she'd sketch the outfits worn by the actors in whatever film they'd seen. She always added her own special touches, which were now known in the industry as the Ingram Flair. Fashion titans couldn't always describe it, but were fond of saying, "You know it when you see it."

But the client hadn't seen it. The up-and-coming producer who wanted wardrobe ideas for a new play didn't care about the Ingram Flair or who had contributed what to the collaboration. Presley doubted he even knew there'd been a collaboration.

She slipped on her jacket and gloves. She went downstairs again and out the door to the rear of the mansion. There was no need to dwell on her colleague's betrayal. She'd already decided not to pursue any legal recourse. But her resolve didn't lessen the pain.

"Any way I can turn that frown upside down?" Trent tapped Presley's elbow with his as he came up beside her.

The gesture and his cheerful voice caused her to smile.

"That's better," he said.

"I didn't realize I was frowning."

"Is something wrong?" Trent asked. "I've been told I'm a good listener. My sisters often find comfort right here." He patted his shoulder.

Presley's smile widened, even though the hurt still knotted her stomach. Not just the hurt of betrayal either. She still needed to confront the pain of returning to this place. Of facing the memories she'd buried for so long.

"I hope you weren't the one who made them cry in the first place," she teased.

"And risk my mama tanning my hide?" Trevor asked, sliding into a Southern drawl. "Not me."

Trent had a talent for accents. He'd told her over supper last night that his dad was in the military. Trent and his family had lived all over the United States and also overseas for a couple of years before they settled outside Omaha while he was in high school.

There was no doubt that Trent loved football, but he had other interests too. He'd explained that he'd seen too many players burn through their money and end up with nothing. A few had sustained career-ending injuries while still at a relatively young age. He couldn't prevent an injury, but he was financially prepared for whatever happened. He said he wanted to be a good steward.

His comment had reminded Presley of a sermon she'd once heard when she attended church with her grandparents. Grandpa had wanted to be a good steward too. But the estate his wife had inherited—the estate that was now the Magnolia Harbor Inn—had demanded too much from them.

"Why do I get the feeling you'd rather be alone?" Trent's voice broke into Presley's musings. "I suppose I could walk in a different direction if you want me to."

Presley bit her inner lip. She'd expected to be alone, but as she'd already experienced, being alone meant following her thoughts down trails she didn't want to go. It might be easier to see the grounds with someone else. Even if that someone else wasn't Clint. While she was here, she should consider making new memories to overlay the old ones. Maybe then the old ones wouldn't sting so much.

"I don't mind your company," she said.

"But do you welcome it?" Trent's voice held a playful note, but the expression in his eyes was serious.

Presley smiled. "I do."

His responding smile lifted the gloom from her spirits. She couldn't do any digging with Trent around. Not that she could dig anyway without some kind of tool. But she could at least see the climbing tree again. Reorient herself to where she needed to search.

They chatted about nothing in particular as they followed the path, a new path, past plots of daffodils surrounded by sweet alyssum and azalea bushes covered with red and white blooms. The path ended in a paved circle with a weathered sundial in the center. It had been there for as long as Presley could remember, but there had never been a path leading to it before.

Trent brushed away the plant debris on the top of the sundial with the sleeve of his jacket. He tried to read the message but stumbled over the timeworn Latin words.

"It says, '*Ultima latet ut observentur omnes.*'" Presley pointed to each word as she read the quotation. "It means, 'Our last hour is hidden from us, so that we watch them all.'"

"Interesting philosophy." Trent repeated the Latin words, getting the pronunciation right this time. "How did you know the translation?"

Presley averted her gaze. The hedge surrounding the paved circle took on a new fascination, though she hardly registered what she was seeing. "I must have heard it somewhere," she finally said.

"I'm not sure what to think of it," Trent admitted. "It's saying to make every hour count for something. But it also has this edge. To be on our guard because death could come at any moment."

She shrugged. "I guess it means both."

"To be watchful because this hour may be our last," he said. "And what? To be productive? Purposeful?"

"I like purposeful."

"Okay, we'll go with watchful and purposeful," Trent said. "They're two concepts that aren't opposed to each other, but I'm not sure how easy it is to hold them both at the same time."

"I hate to tell you this," Presley said, "but I didn't excel in philosophy."

"Yet you know this Latin phrase," he reminded her.

She needed to divert his attention away from her and on to something else. "You surprise me, you know."

"Why's that?" Trent asked.

"I guess I didn't expect a famous football star to give much thought to anything except stats and plays," Presley answered. "Yet here you are, deciphering the hidden nuances of an ancient quotation on a sundial."

"Maybe I'm simply following its advice," he said. "To make the most of this moment."

"That's a simpler interpretation than before."

"A reconciliation of the two concepts." Trent pulled his phone from his pocket. "I'm going to take a photo of the inscription. To show my dad and see what he thinks about it."

While he snapped a photo, Presley returned to the opening in the hedge surrounding the sundial. The new pathway and the circular hedge had gotten her sense of direction off-kilter. But since the sundial was here, then the climbing tree was to its left. She was sure of it.

When Trent joined her, she set off across the lawn toward the climbing tree, a sprawling live oak. She maneuvered around a stand of crepe myrtles and a magnolia tree that hadn't been there ten years ago. The closer she got to the live oak's location, the sicker she felt.

It had to be in this direction, so why couldn't she see it? The crown had risen above a trio of slender pines, bordering a copse of sweet gums and maples. Her grandfather had dubbed them the three sisters. When she spied the pines, she quickened her pace.

"Hey!" he called. "Wait up!"

Presley ignored Trent as she rushed through the needled branches. A large stump, no more than a few feet high, stood in a cleared circle. Flowerless vines snaked out of rustic pots, and curves of broken clay jutted out of the ground in artistic patterns. Wooden benches provided seating near flowering shrubs and patches of assorted daylilies that hadn't yet bloomed.

"It's gone." Presley covered her eyes, and in her memory the peals of childish laughter echoed from the limbs of the giant tree.

"What's gone?" Trent asked when he caught up to her.

She didn't trust her voice enough to answer him.

He walked to the stump and ran his hand across the rough surface. "This must have been a massive tree."

Presley swallowed hard. But the disappointment and pain and regret didn't ease. Emotions she didn't understand ricocheted inside her like an out-of-control bullet, tearing at her heart and her spirit. Never in her wildest dreams had it occurred to her that the climbing tree wouldn't be here.

"I like that there's a wildness to this part of the property." Trent's voice, soft and soothing, was like a balm to her grief. "Not everything should be landscaped and manicured."

"No," Presley murmured. "What do you suppose happened to the tree?"

"Maybe it was struck by lightning."

"So it died." Leaving only a remnant behind. That was what she'd done when she left—when she'd been forced to leave—all those years ago. Her heart had died, but she'd left behind a piece of herself. In her scrapbook hidden away in the chimney. In the memory box buried near her favorite tree.

"You've been here before," Trent said quietly. "Haven't you?"

Presley jerked her gaze toward him. "Yes," she admitted.

"Before the Magnolia Harbor Inn was an inn."

It wasn't really a question, but Presley answered anyway. "Yes."

Trent didn't say anything else, as if he instinctively knew she needed a moment to absorb the loss she was feeling. As if he understood that the tree symbolized something deeper to her than a trunk and limbs and branches.

Presley took a couple of deep breaths before joining him at the stump. She pushed a vine away from the surface, then perched on the edge. "How did you know?" She held up her hand before he could answer. "I guess it was obvious. Why else would I have expected the climbing tree to still be here?"

"The climbing tree? I like the sound of that." He sat beside her. "Did you live here?"

"My grandparents did. I visited them every summer." She let out a bittersweet sigh. "My days here were some of the happiest of my childhood."

"I suspected you had a special connection to this place yesterday," Trent said. "When you were taking photos from the road."

"Why didn't you say anything?" Presley asked.

He shrugged. "I try not to get too nosy too soon."

"I'm glad you didn't ask me," she said. "I might have lied."

"Do you lie often?"

"Hardly ever." Presley rubbed her arms as a sudden chill pulsed through her veins. "It's the first time in almost ten years that I've been back. It feels raw somehow. As if I have to hold all those good and happy memories inside myself or they'll be lost forever."

"Or you could share them with your big brother." Trent placed his arm around her shoulder. The gesture seemed companionable and comforting. "Tell me about the climbing tree."

"It was splendid," she said with a smile. "A centuries-old live oak with sprawling branches. Spanish moss dripping from the limbs. We could go so high. Higher than it was safe, I'm sure."

"Who's we?"

Presley clasped her hands together. They were cold despite the gloves she was wearing. "His name is Clint Calloway. He grew up in Magnolia Harbor." She laughed, the warmth of happier days finally pushing against her sadness. "We were practically inseparable."

"He must be glad you're back in town," Trent remarked.

The warmth dissipated. "He doesn't know."

"And you're not going to tell him?"

Presley didn't answer.

"Look, I get it," he said. "Not the specifics, of course. But I know what it's like to leave someone. You want everything to be the same when you return, but it seldom is."

"You've left someone too?"

"Once upon a time, football meant more to me than anything. Or anyone." Trent pressed his palm against his upper leg as if to rub the soreness out of a muscle. Or perhaps a hurt from someplace deep within. "Eventually she married, and now she has a family."

"I'm sorry," she murmured.

"Don't be," he said. "I think we're both okay with how things turned out."

They sat in silence for a few moments, both lost in their own thoughts.

"Maybe you should give Clint a call," Trent suggested, breaking the silence. "Let him know you're here."

"I can't," Presley replied.

"Sure you can."

"No, it's been too long." Perhaps she could contact Clint if she'd been able to tell him what had happened. But now it was too late.

"If you didn't come back to see Clint and you specifically want to avoid seeing him, then why are you here?"

Presley's cheeks warmed. "You'll think I'm silly."

"Probably not," he said.

"Okay, here goes." Presley took a deep breath. "My mother sent me an e-mail about Clint's engagement. She wanted to be sure I knew he'd forgotten me." She hadn't intended to allow bitterness to seep into her voice. Trent's comforting shoulder seemed to elicit confidences.

"That's cruel," he said.

"I don't want to see him," she continued, "but I needed to come back. To stay in my old room again and visit the places we—I—loved best. Like the climbing tree."

"I'm sorry it's gone."

"Me too." The old tree had always been solid. Strong. Presley had never expected it to fall. But then she'd once thought the same about her and Clint. Yet at the first storm, she hadn't been strong. Instead, she'd let her mother's demands wear her down until she had no substance of her own. Why had she been so weak? So foolish?

Because she'd been young. Not yet nineteen. And her mother's reasons, at least a few of them, were valid.

"How can you and Clint possibly know what you want?" her mother had demanded. "You just graduated high school. You can't give up your scholarships, your dreams. College comes first. After you graduate, then you can think about marriage."

Presley abruptly stood, and her mother's voice fled, leaving her chilled and weary.

Trent rose beside her, and they started walking back to the inn.

They were almost to the rear veranda when Trent said, "I know you came here to find some kind of peace. But you can't spend every day up in the attic. Like that girl. What was her name? Sara something."

Presley couldn't help but smile. "Do you mean Sara Crewe from *A Little Princess*?"

"That's the one. My youngest sister loved that movie. I don't know how many times we had to watch it to keep her happy. Her name is Sara, so I think she hoped that someday she'd wake up and find we were all a dream and that she lived in a fairy-tale castle."

"You don't need to worry about me," Presley said. "I have a very nice and comfortable suite. Nothing like the room Sara Crewe was forced to live in."

"I'm sure you do," Trent said. "But you still can't spend all your time there."

"I won't," she promised, but she didn't know exactly how she would fill her days.

"Go with me to supper tonight," he said. "Dean invited me to The Tidewater, and I don't want to show up alone."

"I don't know."

"You'd be doing me a favor," Trent persisted. "And getting what promises to be an amazing meal."

Presley considered the offer. She could go out with Trent to a nice restaurant or stay up in her room and mope.

"You don't want me to look like I can't get a date, do you?" He made a pitiful face. "Please say yes."

Presley laughed. "Yes."

"Great. I'll make the reservations." Trent pulled out his phone, tapped the screen until he found the number, and made the call.

Presley wandered to a nearby bench. What were the odds that Clint would also be dining at The Tidewater this evening? Exceptionally low, she supposed. Most couples would be planning a romantic Friday night date, not dining out on a Tuesday night. He wouldn't be there.

Instead of feeling reassured, her reasoning added another nick to her brittle heart. She wouldn't go searching for him—she refused to do that. But deep inside she couldn't help wishing that somehow their paths would cross.

Even while she hoped they wouldn't.

12

Presley

A cashmere sweater and designer jeans had been appropriate for last night's supper at Aunt Patsy's Porch. But nothing Presley had brought with her was dressy enough for dinner at The Tidewater. Why hadn't she packed at least one classic black dress? She needed advice.

Winston greeted her when she reached the foyer.

"Hey, little fella." She bent to scratch behind his shaggy brown ears. "Do you know where I can find Grace or Charlotte?"

Winston barked, then scampered toward the kitchen.

Presley followed him, but she hesitated outside the kitchen door. She wasn't sure if guests were welcome in this part of the inn.

Winston sat at her feet and thumped his tail against the floor.

Presley leaned her ear against the door. Someone with a lovely voice was singing a familiar melody. An instant later, Presley recognized it as a song from *Les Misérables*, the one Cosette sang as a little girl.

Presley put her hand on the knob, but she paused before opening the door.

Winston let out an encouraging yip, and the singer stopped.

"Thanks a lot, Winston," Presley muttered. She opened the door and found Charlotte decorating miniature red velvet cupcakes with buttercream frosting. "Hope I'm not interrupting anything."

"Not at all. Come on in." Charlotte set her decorating bag on the counter and wiped her hands on a cloth. "Would you like a glass of iced tea or lemonade?"

"No thanks." Presley rested her hands on the island. "I need advice." Charlotte's eyes widened, and she gestured toward a stool. "I'm all ears."

Presley sat down. "Trent invited me to The Tidewater this evening—"

"Oh, really?"

Presley held up her hands. "As a friend. But I didn't pack a dress, and now I need one."

"You should see Sophie Mah. She runs Miss Millie's dress shop on Main Street." Charlotte picked up the decorating bag and swirled frosting on a cupcake. "She has a fine selection. I'm sure you'll find something there."

"Sophie Mah. Miss Millie's dress shop. Main Street." Presley tapped a rhythm on the island. "Got it. Thank you."

"Anytime." Charlotte grinned. "I hope you find the perfect dress for your friend date."

Presley pretended to glare at her, then got up and left the kitchen.

Presley parked in the closest spot she could find to the dress shop. Before getting out of the car, she peered through the windshield. What if Clint was somewhere nearby right this minute? What if she saw him?

Even worse, what if he saw her?

As if Clint would be shopping inside Miss Millie's.

She scanned the sidewalks but didn't see anyone resembling him. She scolded herself for being ridiculous and got out of the car.

On her way into the store, Presley paused to inspect the window display. Several attractive dresses and outfits adorned the mannequins.

A sense of relief flowed through her. Sophie Mah definitely had an eye for fashion and sophistication.

As Presley entered, a bell over the door chimed.

A woman wearing a trendy garnet dress with black boots stepped from behind the counter. "Welcome to Miss Millie's," she said with a gracious smile. Then her eyes narrowed. "Are you—no, it's not possible, is it?"

"I don't know." Presley's shoulders tensed. *Who does this woman think I am?* "I'm looking for Sophie Mah. Charlotte Wylde suggested I come here."

"You're a guest at the inn?" Something more than polite curiosity tinged the woman's voice.

"That's right. I'm dining at The Tidewater tonight, and I don't have anything to wear. I thought a classic black dress would be appropriate."

The woman eyed her, seeming to evaluate the cut of Presley's jeans and the quality of her ribbed sweater. "I'm Sophie, and I believe I have the perfect dress for you."

Before Presley could respond, Sophie disappeared among the racks.

While Presley waited, she browsed the jewelry in the glass case near the counter. A bold necklace would add a stylish touch to a simple black dress.

Sophie returned with her find. The knee-length crepe sheath was a lovely shade of deep blue with a defined waist. A matching floral lace adorned the bodice and sleeves.

"That's one of mine," Presley breathed.

"I knew it." Sophie laughed in delight. "You're Presley Ingram. I love your style. The Ingram Flair. I can't believe you're in my shop."

"I can't believe you carry my line," Presley said.

"We may not be as high class as New York," Sophie said. "But—"

"No, that's not what I meant," Presley said, rushing to explain.

"I'm honored that you have my clothes when there are so many other lines that you could choose. You even recognized me. No one outside of New York recognizes me."

"I doubt that's true." Sophie proudly held up the dress. "Will a Presley Ingram do for The Tidewater?"

"It's perfect."

"Wonderful." Sophie hesitated. "Though I don't feel comfortable charging you for a dress you designed."

"I'd feel worse if you didn't." Presley gave her a reassuring smile. "I hope you'll carry even more of my designs."

Sophie beamed. "As many as I can. Is there anything else I can help you with?"

"All the accessories."

With Sophie's assistance, Presley selected sapphire earrings, a sapphire-and-diamond bracelet, and black heels. She also purchased a pair of boots, a sweater, and two scarves.

Then Presley remembered that she'd promised to buy something for Shiloh while she was away. A gingham-beaded necklace with matching ball-drop earrings caught her eye. The navy-blue ribbon formed a cloth chain and alternated gingham balls with gold ones. It was exactly the style of unique and fun jewelry that Shiloh loved.

Sophie carefully wrapped all the items except for the dress. "As soon as it's pressed, I'll have it delivered to the inn."

"That would be great," Presley said. "You're a lifesaver."

"And you'll be the loveliest woman there tonight," Sophie said. "Your date is a lucky man."

"He's a friend," Presley clarified.

Sophie practically smirked as she gave Presley a knowing look.

I give up. Presley took the bag, thanked Sophie again, and left the shop.

As she neared her car, she stopped. Trent was leaning against her rental car, his nose buried in his phone. Presley unlocked the car doors with the remote.

Trent jumped at the sound. "Hey." He pocketed the phone and took the bag containing the boots. "Let me help you with that."

"What are you doing here?" Presley asked.

"I saw the BMW and knew you'd return to it sometime." A mischievous gleam appeared in his eyes. "So I decided to wait."

"I'm almost afraid to ask why."

"I was hoping you'd go with me to check out a piece of property I might be interested in buying," Trent said. "It's a few miles west of town."

"Are you moving here?" she asked. Or maybe he wanted a vacation home. This area would be a wonderful place for one.

"Not exactly." He tilted his head toward the SUV parked behind her. "Come with me, and I'll tell you all about my plan."

"Sounds interesting." *And strange.* But Presley didn't have anything else to do. She clicked the lock button on the BMW's remote. "Let's go."

They stashed her purchases in the back seat of his vehicle and climbed in.

As Trent started the ignition, he handed her a cup from the console. "I got you a hot chocolate."

She picked up the cup and read the logo. "The Dragonfly Coffee Shop. Cute name."

"It's right there." He pointed at a small shop. "Owned by a guy named Josh Ford. Rides his bike everywhere and doesn't know a stranger."

"I think the same can be said about you." Presley took a sip of her drink. "This is delicious. Thank you."

"Thank Josh. It was on the house." Trent pulled out of the parking space and followed Main Street. "What did you find at the dress shop?"

"You'll have to wait and see."

"Gladly." He waggled his eyebrows at her.

Presley grinned at his silliness, then took another sip of the hot chocolate and focused on the buildings they passed. She recognized the library, the church, and the park. But much of the town was a blur of businesses and homes. She and Clint had roamed this town every summer.

How could she have forgotten so much of it? Or had that much changed about a place she had loved so well?

13

Clint

Clint erased the line he had just made on his notepad, attempted another one, and broke the lead from his pencil. The broken lead smeared the work he'd already done. With a groan, he wadded up the paper and tossed it toward the net hanging over the wastebasket in the corner. The paper hit the rim and bounced onto the floor.

It seemed like he couldn't do anything right today.

If the wedding hadn't been called off, in three days he would have been dressing in the tuxedo that Margot had chosen. The black one with the crimson vest and bow tie. It wasn't his taste at all, but a Valentine's Day wedding required as much red as possible. At least Margot seemed to think so.

But he hadn't really minded. The details of the wedding had been more important to her than to him. Until they weren't.

Clint pushed away from his desk and wandered to the window. His current project would have to wait. He couldn't concentrate on designing a memorial garden with this strange restlessness surging through his limbs. He swung his arms back and forth, getting the blood flowing, but that didn't quell the agitation roiling in his stomach.

Maybe a breath of fresh air would settle his nerves.

He pocketed his cell phone and grabbed his jacket. "I'm headed to the Dragonfly," he said to Bonnie when he stopped at her desk. "Can I get you something? My treat."

"I'd love a cappuccino," she answered. "And a honey muffin since you're buying."

"You've got it." Clint slid on his jacket and walked out the front door. There weren't too many people roaming the sidewalks of Magnolia Harbor on this sunny Tuesday afternoon. *Give it another day or two.* Every holiday seemed to bring in tourists.

After checking both ways for traffic, he trotted across the street and down the block to the coffee shop. A bell dinged as he opened the door.

Josh Ford, the shop's owner, raised his hand in greeting. "One Americano coming right up."

"Hold it a minute." Clint scanned the available options on the menu board. "Surprise me."

Josh's eyes widened. "Sorry. I thought you were one of my regulars. Clint Calloway. Restorer of gardens and walking plant encyclopedia. Ever meet him?"

"I'm just in the mood for something different today," Clint said.

"One something different coming up." Josh grabbed a marker and wrote *CC* on a coffee cup. "We have fresh chocolate croissants. Want one of those?"

"Why not? I've got an order from Bonnie too." Clint told Josh what Bonnie wanted while he retrieved his debit card from his wallet. Then he gazed around the seating area. A couple of the tables were taken up by strangers, but Glen Abrams, the pastor of Fellowship Christian Church, sat alone in a corner.

Glen waved when he noticed Clint.

"Hey, Pastor. Mind if I join you?"

"Please do." Glen's white Einstein hair contrasted with his lively brown eyes.

Clint turned back to Josh. "I'll be over there."

Josh nodded.

Clint sat down opposite Glen, who set down his e-reader and greeted him with a warm smile.

"I hope I'm not interrupting anything important," Clint said.

"Not at all," Glen said. "The words will still be there when I get back to it."

"I suppose they will." He shifted in his seat. "Nice bit of weather we've been having. Especially for this time of year."

"Penny was saying the same thing at breakfast this morning," Glen said, referring to his wife. "She's itching to get in the garden. In fact, I've been wondering what to get her for Valentine's Day, and now I know. If you'll agree, that is."

Clint chuckled. It wasn't like the well-spoken pastor to be inarticulate. "What am I agreeing to?"

"An hour or two of your time to visit Penny's garden." Glen grew more animated. "She's been studying all these magazines, cutting out pictures of this and that. Benches. Gnomes. Stepping stones. Tall plants. Short plants. If you could come to the house, take a peek at the backyard, and listen to her ideas, then maybe you could make more sense of them than I can. What do you say? I'll pay you, of course."

"Let it be my Valentine's Day gift to both of you," Clint offered.

"That won't do. Then I still won't have a gift for my lovely bride." His face colored. "What am I saying? I didn't mean to be so insensitive. I'm sorry."

"Don't be," Clint said. "I think it's great that you still think of Penny as your bride after . . . How many years has it been?"

"Going on thirty-seven."

Clint was spared from responding when Josh appeared with his order. "Thanks," Clint said. After Josh walked away, Clint took a careful sip of the hot coffee. It tasted exactly like his usual Americano. *Thanks a lot.*

"How are you holding up?" Glen asked.

"I'm fine."

Glen gave him a don't-lie-to-me look.

"I really am," Clint insisted.

"And Margot?" Glen asked. "Have you heard from her?"

"I talked to her a couple of weeks ago. She seems to be settling into her new place. Her new job. I think she likes it out there."

"If you want to get away for a few days, Penny and I would be glad to keep an eye on Donnie for you. It might be nice for you to take a little trip."

"I appreciate the offer," Clint said. "But I've got plenty of work to keep me busy. Besides, Donnie gets home tomorrow, and I'll be spending time with him so I can hear all about his adventures."

Hope Shelter, where Clint's brother, Donnie, lived, had taken him and several other residents on a short trip to the coast.

"You know, if you're feeling any regrets, any resentment even, it would be better to talk it out than to hold it inside," Glen said gently. "We can talk at the church if you'd like more privacy."

"I'm not sure what I feel," Clint admitted. "I guess I should be more disappointed. More hurt. If I feel anything at all, it's guilt that I'm not more upset about it than I am." He picked at his croissant. "That doesn't make any sense."

"Why aren't you more upset?" Glen asked.

"Because I . . . I think I'm relieved." Clint frowned. "Not that it doesn't still hurt that Margot cared more about her career than about Donnie and me."

"And you cared more about Donnie's happiness than your own. Or hers."

"I couldn't take him away from Hope Shelter," Clint said. "It's all he knows. And I couldn't move to the other side of the country and leave him here alone either. He's content. He's thriving. But I need to be close by."

"You do. You do . . ." Glen's voice faded as he repeated the words. "Donnie is very blessed to have a brother like you."

"I'm the one who's blessed," Clint said.

The bell above the door jingled, and Winnie Bennett walked in. She approached their table and greeted them.

"Would you like to join us?" Glen asked her.

"No thank you," Winnie said. "I was on my way to Spool & Thread when I decided to pop in here for a moment." She rummaged through her bag. "Ah, here they are." She handed two tickets to Clint.

"What are these?" he asked.

"Wednesday is Palentine's Night at the theater," she replied. "The idea is to go to the movies with your family and friends. They're showing *The Princess Bride* along with a few other classics. I thought you might like to take Donnie."

"That's very kind of you," Clint said. "Are you sure you and Gus don't want to go?"

"I have a couple other projects that are keeping me too busy for a night at the cinema," Winnie said. "Besides, the last time we went to the movies, Gus decided to take a nap." She laughed. "I thought we'd get kicked out because of his snoring."

"Thank you," Clint said. "Donnie loves that movie. He can quote way too much dialogue from it. Makes you wonder why it's so hard for him to do certain things."

"God's ways are mysterious," Winnie murmured. "Oh, I know that's been said so many times it's become a cliché. Yet look at your sweet brother. I've heard him recite long passages of Scripture too. If that's not proof of God's mysterious plans, I don't know what is. Enjoy the film." With a wave, she bustled out of the shop.

Clint slipped the tickets into his pocket. "A movie with my brother instead of the bridal party dinner Margot had planned. I can't say I'm sorry." It seemed like Margot had planned an event of some kind for every night of the week leading up to the wedding.

"You've got my number if you change your mind about wanting to talk," Glen reminded him.

"Thanks. Guess I'd better get this coffee back to Bonnie before it gets any colder." Clint put his cup in the carrier with the other one and picked up the bag holding her muffin. "When do you want me to stop by to talk to Penny?"

"Whenever you've got the time," Glen answered. "I'll make up some kind of gift certificate for her."

"We can do that at the office," Clint said. "Stop by anytime."

"I'll walk back with you now, if that's all right with you," Glen said.

"Glad for the company." Clint led the way to the door. "But I promise that you don't need to worry about me. I'm fine."

"I know you are," Glen said. "But it never hurts to have a friend nearby in case you aren't."

A shortage of friends didn't seem to be Clint's problem. At least not in this town. Yesterday morning, both Luke and Molly had expressed concern in their own way. Today it was Glen and Winnie. He'd been right to stay here instead of following Margot to California.

Magnolia Harbor was home. It would always be home.

14

Presley

A slight breeze brushed Presley's bare neck, causing a shiver to race down her spine as she stepped onto the veranda for Tuesday evening's hospitality hour. She'd put her hair in a casual updo so she wouldn't have a tangled mess to brush out before going to dinner at The Tidewater. The dress she'd bought from Miss Millie's was waiting for her when she and Trent returned from town. Sophie had even included a sweet personal note thanking Presley for coming to the shop.

Grace introduced Presley to a petite older woman whose eyes sparkled with spunky exuberance. "This is Winnie Bennett, my aunt. Her husband, Gus, is next to the food table talking to Trent."

"Where else would he be?" Winnie said with a laugh. "That man loves to eat, and he loves football." She clasped Presley's hand. "We are so happy to have you visiting with us."

"Thank you," Presley replied. "It's nice to get away from the city for a few days."

"I hope we get a chance to talk again while you're here," Winnie said. "I'm late for my weekly Busy Bees meeting so I've got to run."

"Busy Bees?" Presley asked.

"My quilting club. And dear friends."

After Winnie left, Trent caught Presley's eye and gestured for her to join him. He stood at the buffet table with Grace's uncle and a tall, older man with salt-and-pepper hair.

"Presley, these gentlemen are Gus Bennett and Spencer Lewis.

Spencer is retired FBI." Trent shifted his gaze to the men. "Presley's a famous fashion designer."

"Not famous." She shook the men's hands. "He's exaggerating."

"I've never met a fashion designer before—famous or otherwise," Spencer said. "It's nice to meet you, Presley."

"You too. Thank you."

Trent handed her a plate. "Our reservation at The Tidewater is at seven thirty."

"I don't want to eat too much then," Presley said, studying the offerings. A gorgeous antipasto platter with glistening peppers, gem tomatoes, and olives in every shade adorned a white platter. A mouthwatering variety of cheeses and dried fruit nestled beside piles of thinly sliced ham and mortadella. A cloth-lined basket held a collection of crackers and breads. "Though everything looks delicious."

"Charlotte's an amazing chef," Spencer said. "So is Dean. You're sure to enjoy anything he prepares."

"That's great to hear." Presley stacked a piece of Serpa cheese on a delicate water cracker, added a folded slice of ham, and topped it with half a dried apricot. She couldn't resist taking one of the red velvet miniature cupcakes to keep it company.

Grace appeared with a platter of chilled tortellini and shrimp stacked on shiny copper skewers. "Are you men still talking football?" she asked.

"Not since Presley joined us." Trent helped himself to one of the skewers. "I think I told her all my best football stories last night."

"Did you have any of the famous pie at Aunt Patsy's?" Grace asked.

"Yes, and it was amazing," Trent said. "We're going to The Tidewater this evening. Dean promised us a meal we'd never forget."

"I'm sure he'll deliver on that promise," Grace said.

After Presley finished the tasty snacks, she shifted so her back was slightly to Trent, Spencer, and Gus. "I've been admiring the grounds," she said to Grace. "The landscaping is lovely."

"I enjoy working in the gardens," Grace said. "But it seems there's always more to do."

"Surely you don't take care of all this land yourself," Presley said.

"Goodness, no," Grace said with a laugh. "There's a local company that does the routine maintenance and the heavy work."

"Trent and I took a walk this morning," Presley said. "We found an old stump with potted plants and ivy around it."

Grace nodded. "The grandfather stump."

"The grandfather stump?" Presley echoed.

"First it was the grandfather tree because it was so big, and now it's the grandfather stump," Grace explained. "Charlotte named it."

"What happened to it?" Presley asked.

"Some kind of fungus. I forget the technical name for it now. We were talking to a tree expert about what to do, and then we had a tremendous thunderstorm. This was about four, maybe five years ago. The tree was hit by lightning." Grace gave a rueful smile. "It was such a beautiful tree. It still makes me sad to think of it being destroyed."

Presley averted her gaze. Trent had been right. But the tree would have been cut down even if it hadn't been hit by the lightning. It had rotted from the inside. In fact, it had probably been rotting for years. If she had been here, if she had known, could she have done something to save the tree?

Regret tightened her stomach. Another piece of her childhood was gone. Splintered by something no one could control.

Grace touched her arm. "Are you all right?"

Presley turned to her with a forced smile. "I'm fine. Just thinking about the tree. Did you design the garden around the stump?"

"We left all that to Oliver Nichols," Grace replied. "He owns Two

Green Thumbs, our lawn care company. Oliver brought out the nicest young man. He was full of ideas and helped us decide what we wanted. Then Oliver did the rest."

"It's a very peaceful spot," Presley commented. "Secluded."

"It certainly is," Grace said. "But I haven't been out there for a while. I'm sure it needs a bit of tidying up."

"I thought it looked perfect just the way it was," Presley said.

Grace smiled at the compliment, then glanced toward the door as the other inn guests headed their way.

Presley had heard that one couple was celebrating a milestone wedding anniversary, and the other was celebrating their honeymoon. She pushed away the tang of envy that stung her heart. Both couples appeared so happy, so in love with each other.

"You seem to be having fun," Grace said to the newcomers. "There's plenty of food. Hope you're hungry."

"Starving," Justin said. "Especially after climbing to the top of that lighthouse you told us about."

"The view was worth it," Bethany added. "But I'm glad we're spending tomorrow on a boat. I'm not sure I'll be able to get upstairs to our room."

"I told you not to wear those sandals," Justin teased.

"But they're cute," Bethany retorted.

"Everything is cute on you." Justin pulled his wife into a hug.

Presley wandered over to the beverage table. She took a glass of water, then sat down at one of the tables.

As she sipped her water, her thoughts whirled. Grace had mentioned a nice young man who'd advised her on what to do with the area surrounding the stump. Could that have been Clint? The engagement announcement said he was a landscape architect. Presley hadn't been surprised. Back when she'd known him, he could identify practically every plant, flower, and tree that he saw, both the cultivated and the wild.

If it had been Clint, what had he thought about the loss of the climbing tree? Did he feel the same loss she did? Or had he put their childhood rambles behind him when he fell in love with someone else?

Most importantly, had Clint left the box where they'd hidden it? Or had he taken it?

There was only one way to find out. Tonight, after she returned from The Tidewater, she'd do a little digging of her own.

15

Winnie

As soon as the women of The Busy Bees quilting group were settled with their projects at Spool & Thread, Angel Diaz let out a huge sigh.

"What's wrong?" Winnie asked.

"I've been looking forward to this evening all day," Angel said. The talented artist had adorned her hands and arms with henna hearts and vines that disappeared beneath the flowing sleeves of her brightly colored top. "Why do people wait until the last minute to plan their Valentine's Day gifts? I'll never understand it."

"Are you too busy for your own good?" Helen massaged her knuckles. Instead of working on her signature wedding quilt this evening, she held a basket of assorted fabric squares. While the others worked on their own projects, she sorted the squares into collections for Judith to sell in the shop. "It's always like this when Valentine's Day draws near."

"I tried to prepare for it. I really did." Angel shook her head, sending her thick dark ponytail flying. "I created a special selection of valentine-themed illustrations and one-of-a-kind cards. But it's not enough."

"So what's the problem?" Judith asked.

"It's the men," Angel said. "They don't know what they want, and they're afraid of choosing the wrong thing. I feel sorry for them, but they have to make their own decisions." She focused on pinning a vibrant yellow fabric flower to the middle of a four-patch block made up of alternating silver and blue fabrics. The quilt was for her niece's quinceañera party in Tampa at the end of June.

"There's another man who needs our help." Winnie said. "But he's leaving all the decision-making to us."

"That better not be my Joe," Patty Duncan said as she pushed aside a strand of wavy red hair. "I already told him that I want only one thing for Valentine's Day."

"What's that?" Judith asked.

"Can't you guess?" Patty didn't give the other women a chance to answer before she rushed on. "I want him to build the sets for this year's spring classic. You'll never guess what play the theater board has selected. It's going to be absolutely marvelous. I simply can't wait for the big reveal."

"Does that mean you aren't going to tell us?" Angel asked with a grin. "You do like your secrets, don't you?"

"I promised not to say a word," Patty said. "But as soon as we get the green light, you'll be among the first to know. I'm trying out for—" She covered her mouth and giggled. "Oops. I almost let it slip."

Winnie bent over her work to hide her smile. She adored each one of these women and often thanked God for bringing them together every week to enjoy each other's company. Angel, the youngest of the group, brought an artistic flair, but Patty's dramatic talent had its own charm. Patty had been involved in the local theater for years, and her son, Billy—a young Brad Pitt look-alike—could be seen in minor roles in commercials and TV shows.

Judith cleared her throat and faced Winnie. "I didn't realize Dean knew about Grace's plans. I thought she wanted to surprise both him and Charlotte."

"I wasn't talking about Dean." Winnie glanced at Patty. "Or Joe."

"I'm confused," Patty said. "What's this about Grace and a surprise?"

"Grace stopped by yesterday when Winnie and Helen were here," Judith explained. "Because Dean has to work late on Friday, she asked us to plan a Valentine's Day surprise for him and Charlotte."

"So who's the other man who needs our help?" Patty asked.

"Spencer." Winnie basted a butterfly appliqué piece on an ivory square. Her project was a quilt for one of her granddaughters. "I got a text from Charlotte when I was here yesterday. She wanted me to come to the cottage while Grace was away from the inn. Spencer was there too, and he wants advice on planning a surprise for Grace."

"Do you mean they're finally going to be a real couple?" Angel asked.

"I don't know about that," Winnie said. "But it does seem like Cupid is pointing his arrows at hearts all over Magnolia Harbor."

"How exciting." Patty practically jumped up and down in her seat. "Grace and Spencer are so good together. I don't know what's taken them so long to see it for themselves. If their lives were a movie, they'd have fallen in love ages ago."

Winnie held up a hand. "I'm not saying they're in love. Only that Judith, Helen, and I promised Grace we'd plan a surprise for Charlotte, and now Spencer wants help planning a surprise for Grace. And I can't do it by myself."

"Of course we'll do whatever we can," Angel said.

"We'll call it Operation Romance," Patty said. "This is going to be so much fun. Do you have any ideas?" She put her project on the table and retrieved a notebook from her bag. "We need to take notes."

Helen straightened a stack of variegated denim squares and placed them in a box. "Who else is getting hit by Cupid's arrows, Winnie? Someone at the inn?"

"The two single guests seem to be spending time together," Winnie answered. "And I must say, they make a striking couple. Both live in New York. Both are good-looking and successful." She paused to add another stitch. "In fact, the young man is rather famous in the sports world. He's a football player named Trent Jacobs."

Angel almost dropped her quilt on the floor. "Trent Jacobs is staying at the inn? Do you think I could get his autograph for one of my cousins? Felipe has followed his career since he graduated college. He was devastated when the Giants drafted Trent before the Bucs could."

"I don't know about an autograph, but perhaps I could bring you a napkin he used," Winnie teased.

"I'll take it," Angel declared. "Anything. Felipe will owe me big-time."

"I'll see what I can do," Winnie said with a small shake of her head.

"Who's the other single guest?" Judith asked.

"Presley Ingram," Winnie replied. "She's a fashion designer, and apparently she's quite talented."

"The name sounds familiar," Judith said, tilting her head. "Though I'm not very acquainted with the fashion industry."

"Ladies." Patty tapped her pen against her notebook. "We can talk about football and fashion later. Winnie has given us a mission. What are we going to do for Charlotte and Dean and Grace and Spencer? We need to create a backdrop for romance and make this Valentine's Day an evening they'll never forget."

By the time the meeting broke up at Spool & Thread, Operation Romance had been divided into two separate missions. With her usual dramatic flair, Patty had dubbed them Mission Kindle for Spencer and Grace and Mission Glow for Dean and Charlotte.

Winnie wasn't sure what she thought about the names, but Patty and Angel had laughed themselves into hysterics as they suggested and discarded one name after another. Winnie supposed she should be glad they hadn't landed on anything even more bizarre.

She gathered her things and joined in the chorus of goodbyes.

"Any chance you're parked near me?" Judith asked her. "I thought we could walk out together if you don't mind waiting for me to turn out the lights."

"I'm parked close enough," Winnie said. Judith must want to talk to her in private. "And I can wait."

The other women left, and a few moments later, Judith was ready to leave. Winnie followed her out the back door to the rear parking lot.

"I've been thinking about Presley Ingram and where I've heard that name before," Judith said.

"Do you know her?" Winnie asked.

"I'm not sure," Judith said. "Presley is an unusual name, and I can't help wondering if she isn't the same girl."

"The same girl?" Winnie echoed.

"This was years ago when Ken and I first moved here," Judith said. "The woman who lived at the inn—though it wasn't the inn back then—anyway, she was one of the first to welcome me to town. Her granddaughter was visiting for the summer, and she loved to browse in my store. I remember being so pleased. She was about seventeen, and not many teenage girls know as much about fabrics as she did. Maybe that's why I remember her."

As Judith talked, Winnie's own memories seemed to open up. The owners of the mansion had had a granddaughter. She had visited them every summer . . . until one summer she hadn't.

"Her name was Presley Ingram?" Winnie asked.

Judith shook her head. "I don't remember her last name. I'm not sure I even knew it. But, yes. Her first name was Presley."

"I don't think it can be the same girl," Winnie responded. "If she'd said anything to Grace or Charlotte about her grandparents being the former owners, they would have told me."

Though, come to think of it, Grace had mentioned that Presley had been adamant about staying in the Wisteria Loft Suite. But that didn't mean anything, did it? Photos of all the suites were posted on the inn's website. Perhaps it was the suite Presley liked the best. Some guests seemed especially interested in staying in a room on the third floor. It definitely provided more privacy.

"I remember the next year," Judith continued, "her grandmother rarely came into the shop, but I ran into her at the grocery once. I asked about Presley. When she told me that her granddaughter wasn't coming, her voice trembled. I was afraid she was going to cry right there between the tomatoes and the oranges. But she pulled herself together and gave me a sad little smile, then explained that Presley was too busy with college to visit."

"Too busy to visit during summer break?" But who was Winnie to judge? The story pained her heart, but she hadn't known the family well despite them being near neighbors. They'd had a different set of friends and hadn't socialized very much outside of it. Now Winnie remembered the rumors going around that they'd had financial problems.

No wonder they'd had money troubles with that huge house to take care of. It had needed a lot of work when Grace and Charlotte bought it. They probably hadn't had the means to do the needed repairs. But Winnie had been sorry when they died within a few weeks of each other. Even that had been a strange affair. It had been a private funeral and not well attended according to the local gossips.

"My mind is fuzzy on the details, and I haven't thought about this in ages." Judith opened the back door of her car and set her belongings inside. "But it seems to me that when Presley was last here, her mother came to town unexpectedly. She stayed only a day. Maybe two. When she left, Presley went with her. The grandmother apparently hadn't expected her to leave so soon."

"Yes." Winnie searched her memory banks. "I remember hearing something about that now. The mother didn't like it that Presley was friends with one of the local boys."

"I think you're right," Judith said. "Who was he?"

"Oh, it was Clint Calloway," Winnie said. "He and Presley would ride their bikes past our house sometimes."

"The landscaper who got jilted?" Judith asked.

"Yes, Clint the landscaper. But he didn't get jilted." Winnie gave Judith a look. "They were supposed to be married this Friday on Valentine's Day. But they called off the engagement a few months ago."

"She moved to California, didn't she?"

"You're asking me?" Winnie teased. "You're the one who knows everything that goes on in this town."

"I can't help it if people don't lower their voices while they're browsing in my shop," Judith retorted.

Winnie laughed.

"Poor Clint," Judith said. "I was so excited for him when I heard about his engagement. It can't be easy for him, taking care of Donnie the way he does."

"I've never heard him complain," Winnie said.

"Me either. But I did hear that the wedding was called off because he refused to move Donnie from the facility he's in. And Clint didn't want Donnie living here without any family close by."

"That's the same reason I heard." Winnie didn't know Clint well, though he'd grown up in Magnolia Harbor. Shortly after returning to town to open his landscaping company, Grace had hired him to design the heritage garden. She'd been impressed with his knowledge of historic plants. "If the marriage was meant to be, then his bride would have stayed in Magnolia Harbor too. It's probably better they found out before the wedding that they had different priorities."

"Amen to that," Judith said. "If Presley Ingram is the same girl who used to come into my store, maybe she's here to see Clint."

"Perhaps," Winnie said.

But as Winnie drove home, she felt a sense of unease. If the guest at the inn was the same Presley, then why hadn't she told them who she was? What was she hiding?

16

Presley

The hostess at The Tidewater seated Presley and Trent at a secluded table beside one of the large windows so they had a lovely view of the lights shimmering on the lake. Trent, handsome as ever in dark slacks and a sports jacket, was attentive, fun, and engaging—the perfect date. When fans interrupted their meal, he was gracious to them and apologetic to Presley.

Not that she had minded. If anything, she enjoyed the attention he received. Especially after experiencing her own moment of fandom with Sophie Mah earlier in the day. The warm glow of being recognized by someone in a small town so far from New York still lingered within her.

While dining on marinated salmon steaks and antique broccoli, Presley and Trent talked about the property they'd visited earlier in the day. The twenty-acre wooded parcel bordered a meandering stream and was located several miles off the main highway. Trent's vision, inspired by the experiences of his best friend, was to create a retreat where soldiers returning from overseas duty could enjoy an upscale but low-cost vacation with their families.

Presley pointed out that his investment wouldn't make him any money.

Trent leaned forward as if to tell her a secret. "Not all investing is about money. And not all treasure is found here on Earth."

Sometimes the man seemed too good to be true. Presley wanted to support his project in some way, but she hadn't yet figured out how.

Writing a check would be easy, but she wanted to do something more. Something that mattered.

For dessert, they shared a strawberry almond cake roll and bittersweet chocolate truffles served with clementine wedges. The conversation shifted to living in New York, including their favorite sections of Central Park and where to find the best bagels.

Before Presley and Trent left, Dean stopped by their table to see how they were doing. They thanked him and told him how much they enjoyed the food. Given how packed the place was, Presley was touched that Dean had taken the time to check in with them.

When they returned to the inn, Presley said good night to Trent at the foot of the stairs leading to the Wisteria Loft Suite.

He gave her a peck on the cheek, then waited until she was at the top of the stairs and had unlocked her own door before he slipped into his room. A chivalrous and gentlemanly gesture, though it was totally unnecessary here at the inn.

The delicious meal and engaging company had distracted Presley from thoughts of Clint and the reason for her return to Magnolia Harbor. But now that she was back at the inn, she had a job to do.

She slipped out of her dress and changed into black jeans and a dark sweatshirt. After pulling her hair into a messy bun, she studied her reflection and smiled. If she'd had camouflage paint, she might have used it too. The thought amused her and eased the nervous tension in her stomach.

But what did she have to be nervous about? She was only retrieving something that belonged to her. Okay, to her and Clint. But what man would dig up a box holding his childhood memories after marrying someone else? Clint probably hadn't thought of the box again. After all, it had been almost ten years since they'd buried it.

Not wanting to take a chance that Trent would hear her, she forced herself to watch the rerun of a sitcom. Hopefully, he'd be asleep by the time it ended.

As soon as the credits rolled, Presley turned off the television, slipped on her black sneakers, and grabbed the trowel and flashlight she'd purchased before going to the dress shop. Thankfully, the door didn't squeak when she opened it. And it seemed that Grace and Charlotte had repaired the creaky board on the landing that used to give her away when she left her room.

Even so, she took her time descending the stairs. The rooms on the second floor were quiet except for the soft jazz escaping from the Bluebell Suite. She wasn't sure which couple was staying in that room.

Presley quietly made her way to the first floor and paused. All was still, as if the mansion itself slept. Decorative night-lights, strategically placed on the mantel and in electrical outlets near the baseboards, provided enough light so she didn't bump into any furniture. She knew that Grace's living quarters were in the back, so she slipped out the front door.

As Presley crept around the house, she turned on her flashlight. Instead of following the roundabout path to the sundial, she cut across the grounds to the copse where the three sisters stood sentinel.

An owl hooted, and the woods were louder than she'd expected, but she tamped down her fear. She'd come to the woods before at night, sneaking out of the house after her grandparents had gone to bed to meet Clint at the climbing tree. They'd sit in the tree house and share a late-night snack. Or they'd climb on top of the tree house and gaze at the stars through the leafy canopy.

They'd made plans to meet that last night so they could dream about their future together. Instead, Presley had been on a plane to Seattle. Almost as far from Magnolia Harbor as she could get and still be in the United States. Once they arrived at the Seattle airport,

Mother rented a car and drove them to a wilderness cabin where they stayed for two weeks. She locked Presley's phone and laptop in a safe in the cabin's closet.

Mother said they were having a vacation from technology. Something they both needed while they spent time together. Perhaps it would be their last mother-daughter vacation for a while since Presley would be going to college soon. Who knew when they could do it again?

For Presley, it felt more like a kidnapping.

But her mother had her way. Like always. By the time they returned to their Chicago home, Presley had admitted Mother was right. She and Clint were too young to know what they wanted out of life. She couldn't walk away from the scholarships she had received or the prestigious education she was sure to get. Her future was in the fashion houses of New York. She couldn't give up the amazing possibilities that awaited her there for a summer crush.

Though Clint had seemed like so much more.

He still seemed like so much more.

But Clint was married. Or getting married. Either way, he was in love with someone else. A lovely blonde with cute dimples and a sparkle in her eyes.

If only Presley had avoided studying the announcement.

No good had come of that.

When she reached the location, she thrust the trowel into the ground near the stump, even though it wasn't where they'd buried the box. Not this close to the tree. Still, the movement released a bit of the heartache building up inside her. She moved the flashlight beam from side to side and back again.

The spot by the exposed root. That was the place. She was sure of it.

Presley dug and dug.

No box.

Maybe it was on the other side of the stump. She dug there.

Still no box.

It had to be here somewhere. Presley dug four more holes, growing more desperate each time she came up empty.

Finally, she plopped onto the stump and buried her head in her hands. The box wasn't here. That meant she wasn't searching in the right place. Or that the lawn care company had found it. Or that Clint had taken it.

Presley didn't know which of the latter two options bothered her more.

She dug three more holes without success. Tears welled up in her eyes, but she refused to cry.

Grace had told her that the tree had been cut down four or five years ago. Even though Presley knew it was a long shot, she decided to locate the lawn care company and talk to the owner. If his company had found the box, maybe he still had it. Or maybe he would know what happened to it.

She could only hope he hadn't thrown it away. Or given it to Clint.

Because if Clint had it, she'd never see it again.

Presley

Presley pulled the key to the rental car from the ignition and glanced at Trent. Even though he'd pushed the passenger seat as far back as it would go, his knees were almost to his chin.

Earlier that morning, after she had skipped breakfast, Trent appeared at her door with a banana-nut muffin and a travel mug of hot chocolate. Comforted by his brotherly concern, she told him about the memory box and her late-night search. He'd said all the right things and encouraged her to make this stop.

"Are you sure you don't mind going in there with me?" she asked.

"Nothing I'd rather do." Trent cracked open his door and slid one leg out without taking his eyes off Presley. "Besides, we already talked about this. I go to your meeting with you, and you go to my meeting with me. Then lunch."

"As long as it's my treat this time," Presley insisted.

"You've got it. Just please don't take me to one of those places with nothing but salads and dainty teacups."

Presley tilted her head. "My grandparents used to take me to a BBQ place nearby. How would that be?"

"My mouth is already watering." Trent pulled himself from the car and shut the door.

Presley rested her palm on the door handle, then peered through the windshield at the people on the sidewalk. A knot formed in her stomach as she searched for a familiar face. For one familiar face in particular. But Clint wasn't with the group of guys walking down the street or the woman window-shopping.

She experienced the same feelings she'd had yesterday. Fear of seeing him. Disappointment that she hadn't.

A rap sounded on the passenger window, and she turned.

Trent grinned at her through the glass and beckoned.

Presley opened the door, stepped out, and glanced at the storefront sign. *Two Green Thumbs.* She'd called the lawn care company after breakfast to talk to the owner, Oliver Nichols. He wasn't available at the time, but she'd been able to make an appointment. There was no reason to be nervous. All she needed to do was ask a couple of questions. She could do this.

"Ready?" Trent asked.

"Sure." Presley took a deep breath and squared her shoulders.

Together they entered the office.

A woman sat behind a desk littered with papers and files. "Welcome to Two Green Thumbs," she said cheerily. "I'm Elaina Nichols. What can I do for you?"

Presley stepped closer to the desk. "I'm here to see Mr. Nichols. I called earlier."

"Oh yes. He's in the back. Right through those doors." Elaina pointed to an open doorway leading to a short hall. "All the way to the end."

"Thank you," Presley said.

Trent led the way down the hall.

Presley wrinkled her nose as the pungent odors became stronger. "Not the most pleasant place to work, is it?" she said softly to him.

"Chemicals and fertilizer, I guess."

"Some kind of fuel too."

Trent shrugged. "Tools of the trade."

"Too bad it can't smell like freshly mown grass and gardenias," Presley mused.

"Or freshly painted lines and Astroturf." He grinned. "I can't get enough of those smells."

She chuckled.

Trent pushed through the heavy door leading to a large open space that reminded Presley of a huge garage. A truck was parked to one side, and a riding mower sat on a trailer next to the truck. Worktables, storage shelves, and an assortment of equipment were arranged in a somewhat haphazard manner on the other side.

A middle-aged man with sandy-blond hair and blue eyes stood behind a long wooden table as he transferred seedlings to a larger planter. When Presley and Trent approached, he wiped his hands on a cloth and smiled at them in welcome. "I don't believe it. You're Trent Jacobs, aren't you? Right here in my shop." He extended a hand to him.

"I sure am." Trent shook his hand, then introduced Presley. "You must be Mr. Nichols. We're glad to meet you."

"Please call me Oliver. What are you doing way down here?" He grinned. "You know, we wouldn't mind if you came to play for the Carolina Panthers."

"I'll keep that in mind if I'm ever unhappy with the Giants," Trent replied with a chuckle. "Magnolia Harbor does seem like a great place to call home."

"Not planning to move here, are you?" Oliver asked.

"Maybe someday." Trent gestured to Presley, making her feel like she was part of the conversation. "Ms. Ingram has a couple questions she'd like to ask you."

"Of course." Oliver faced Presley. "You must be the woman who called earlier. How can I help you?"

Presley forced a smile. Why couldn't she get her nerves under control? This was a simple conversation, yet she was as tense as if it was the opening night of Fashion Week. "I'm staying at the Magnolia Harbor Inn," she began.

"Very nice," Oliver said. "I'm sure Grace and Charlotte are treating you well."

"They definitely are." Presley resisted the urge to wipe her sweaty palms on her trousers. "Grace said you planted the garden near the old tree that got struck by lightning. Did you happen to find anything when you were digging?"

Oliver cocked his head. "Like what?"

"A metal box," she said.

"Was there a metal box buried near that tree?" Oliver asked.

"There might have been."

Oliver seemed to study Presley's face. She didn't flinch from his scrutiny, but she was almost sure he wouldn't know who she was. She didn't remember ever meeting him during the summers she spent with her grandparents.

"I know it sounds strange," Trent said to Oliver. "But if you found something, Ms. Ingram would be very grateful. So would I."

"It's been several years, but I don't recall finding anything out of the ordinary." Oliver frowned as if he were sorry he couldn't help his hero. "I wish I had."

Presley smiled to hide her disappointment. "Grace said she hired a landscape designer for the project. Do you remember who that was?"

"I *can* help you with that one." Oliver seemed to breathe a sigh of relief.

Presley felt slightly amused at the man's eagerness. Oliver was obviously a kind and friendly man, probably the best of neighbors too. But having Trent along seemed to give everyone they met a bit of added incentive to exhibit the famous Southern hospitality.

"I wanted the job to go to Clint Calloway," Oliver said.

Presley involuntarily stiffened at the mention of Clint's name, and Trent rested a comforting hand on her shoulder.

"He's a local guy," Oliver continued. "Went off to college, then came back here to open his own business. But he didn't want the job. I never understood why he turned it down. Not that it made much difference. He's certainly doing well for himself." He chuckled. "I'm sorry. I didn't mean to go on like that. You don't want to hear about Clint."

Yes, I do. Presley shuddered. *No, I don't.* Though it might have been best for Oliver to talk a little bit longer. To have mentioned Clint's wedding and to say how ecstatic the newlyweds were. She didn't want to know such things, but perhaps hearing them from a stranger would be good for her. As it was, she nodded politely and pretended that her heart wasn't tearing her apart.

"So, who did the design work?" Trent asked.

Presley shot him a thankful smile.

"Clint had a mentor in Charleston who came out and gave Grace and Charlotte what they wanted," Oliver said. "He did a fine job."

"Do you remember his name?" Trent asked.

"No, but I should have it on here." Oliver drew his phone from a pocket and tapped the screen. "Austin Price. Do you need his number?"

"That would be great." Trent pulled out his phone. After the contact info had been shared, he clapped Oliver on the back. "Thanks for your time. We appreciate it."

Oliver turned his gaze to Presley. "I'm sorry I didn't have better news about the box."

"It's not important," she said, giving him a warm smile.

Oliver walked with them to the front office. "I know you met my wife, Elaina, when you walked in." He turned to Elaina. "Do you know who this is? Trent Jacobs. He plays for the New York Giants."

Elaina's eyes widened, and then she gave them both a warm smile. "My husband's a big football fan."

Presley thought it was the perfect diplomatic answer.

"I don't suppose . . . I mean, would you mind if we took a photo together?" Oliver asked.

"Not at all," Trent said graciously.

"I'll take it for you," Presley offered.

Oliver thanked her and handed over his phone. She snapped a couple of photos, and Elaina provided a piece of paper for Trent to autograph.

When they were back in the car, Presley put the key in the ignition. "They're a nice couple, but I don't know how you deal with that attention day after day."

"You get used to it," Trent said. "Actually, living in New York makes it easier. I'm not that big of a deal because there are so many celebrities there."

"But outside of New York?"

He shrugged. "It feels kind of good. I plan to enjoy it while I can because I know it won't last forever."

"I have a feeling Oliver Nichols will never forget you," Presley said.

"Maybe not. But there's a new crop of players each year, and they all want to make a name for themselves. I won't always be a fan favorite."

Presley drove to their next destination, an attorney's office. Trent had an appointment to discuss the procedure for setting up a nonprofit organization to oversee his project. Before they went into the lobby, he sent her the contact info for Austin Price.

While Trent was in his meeting, Presley called the number.

To her surprise, Austin answered. Apparently, Oliver had given them the man's cell phone number instead of an office number.

Presley quickly recovered and asked about the Magnolia Harbor

Inn project. Austin remembered designing the garden, but he didn't recall finding anything. Presley thanked him and ended the call.

As she waited for Trent, she flipped through a couple of magazines in the lobby, but she couldn't concentrate on the articles.

Maybe she hadn't dug in the right place. But how could she have forgotten the location of something so important?

Presley didn't want to consider the only other answer she could think of, but she had no choice. What if Clint had broken their agreement and retrieved the box? If the situation had been reversed, if she was the one still living in Magnolia Harbor when the tree was destroyed and the ground was going to be dug up, she definitely would have taken the box before anyone else could find it.

Clint had to have it. And if he did, there was nothing she could do.

Not unless she faced him

Presley cringed, imagining how humiliating it would be to talk to him again, especially after the way she'd left him. He was happy, successful, and in love. She was brokenhearted, and her career was falling apart.

Seeing him would take more courage and strength than she possessed.

And yet she needed to know, without a doubt, what had happened to the memory box.

Grace

After folding a load of towels and placing them in the linen closet, Grace headed to the kitchen. Spencer had stopped by the hospitality hour last night, but he'd seemed more interested in their famous football player than spending time with Grace. A couple of opportunities had opened up for them to chat, but each time he seemed distracted. Had the trip to Charleston to see *Les Misérables* been an ending instead of a beginning? Or maybe God's plan was for them to remain good friends.

She could be content with that. Couldn't she?

Grace pushed the question from her mind. No need to think about romance—or the lack of it—when she had a million other things to contemplate. Like the grandfather stump. The original design was for a restful retreat, similar to a meditation or prayer garden. But it was tucked away in the woods, and she realized it was a case of out of sight, out of mind.

She entered the kitchen and started tidying up.

Charlotte came in through the back entry with a laptop under one arm and a large tote bag slung over her shoulder. "Are you ready for lunch? I made chicken salad and pickled dill beans with cheddar cheese."

"When was the last time you were out at the grandfather stump?" Grace asked.

Charlotte placed her laptop on the island. "Is that a no for lunch?"

"Sorry. Lunch sounds great, but could we postpone it for a bit?"

"Sure." Charlotte tilted her head in thought. "And to answer your question, I have no idea. Why?"

"Last night during the hospitality hour, Presley mentioned that she and Trent had been out there," Grace explained. "Since then, it's been on my mind to see how it fared through the winter."

"I'm up for a walk. Let's go."

The women left by the back door.

Winston, relaxing in a patch of sunshine on the porch, lifted his head.

"Want to join us?" Grace asked.

He barked once, then trotted to her.

She smiled and scratched behind his ears.

The threesome set off toward the woods.

"I think we've burned most of the wood we got from that old tree," Charlotte said. "When was the storm?"

"Four or five years ago." Grace veered from the path and cut across the lawn toward the woods. "I was surprised when Presley brought it up. It's been a long time since I knew of any of our guests going out there."

"We don't do a very good job of telling people about it," Charlotte said. "Maybe that's why it's not more popular."

"Maybe."

"Why were Presley and Trent out there?" Charlotte asked.

"She didn't say. But she was curious about who did our lawn care. And who designed the landscaping."

"Perhaps she's searching for inspiration." Charlotte laughed. "I can see it now. A line of clothing stamped with the image of the grandfather stump."

Grace laughed too. "If that happens, I'll buy you a T-shirt."

Winston ran on ahead, disappearing into the copse of trees. When he returned, he had dirt on his snout.

Grace scooped him up and brushed away the dirt. "Oh, Winston. Don't tell me you were digging in the garden. You know that's not allowed."

The dog yipped.

Grace set Winston down, and they continued toward the stump.

"I don't think it was Winston," Charlotte said. She pointed to several spots where the soil had been turned. "Someone's been digging."

Grace frowned. "Why would anyone do that?"

"I see at least seven places," Charlotte said as she wandered around the stump.

Winston followed her, sniffing the holes.

Grace knelt beside the largest spot and pressed her fingers into the soil. It had definitely been disturbed.

"Do you suppose Presley and Trent did this?" Charlotte asked.

Grace glanced at her sister. "Why would they?"

"I have no idea," Charlotte said. "But they're the only ones we know who were here."

"You're right." Grace stood and brushed the dirt from her fingers. "If that's the case, then why would Presley tell me she was here?"

"She didn't know you'd come to check," Charlotte pointed out.

"But she didn't know I wouldn't."

Charlotte sat on the edge of the stump. "What was the digger searching for? And did he or she find it?"

"Apparently not where the person expected to." Grace waved her hand to encompass the garden. "Otherwise, there wouldn't be so many holes."

"At least it's something that can be fixed," Charlotte said.

"True." Grace pulled out her cell phone. "The plants need attention anyway. I'll give Oliver a call."

19

Clint

After placing his order with Angel, Clint chose a table by the window. Pastor Glen had called him that morning to see if they could meet. Apparently, he'd managed to get his hands on Penny's dream garden notebook, and he hoped Clint could take a peek at it before meeting with her.

Clint figured he could just as easily have gone through the notebook with Penny, but the pastor's excitement over his surprise Valentine's Day gift was contagious. Bonnie had already created a special gift certificate for Glen to present to his wife on Friday. Bonnie had also arranged, with Glen's go-ahead, for Angel to create a plaque that could be included in the garden's design. The plaque would commemorate the occasion with the date and a special message from Glen.

The bell to the coffee shop's door jingled, drawing Clint's attention. He expected to see Pastor Glen.

But Oliver Nichols stepped through the door and glanced around. He acknowledged Clint with a raised finger, then waited as Angel placed Clint's coffee and pastry on the counter.

Clint started to rise.

"I'll bring it to you," Oliver said to Clint. "If you don't mind me joining you."

"Don't mind at all." Clint settled back into his seat. "As long as Angel puts whatever you're getting on my tab."

"No need for that," Oliver said.

"I insist." He drew a bill from his wallet. Oliver was a good friend, and Clint appreciated all the work the landscaper had sent his way when he opened his business. During those first lean months, Oliver had even hired Clint to be part of his crew.

Oliver chatted a moment with Angel, placed his order, then brought Clint his coffee and pastry. "Keeping busy?" he asked as he took a seat across from Clint.

"It's still a little slow, but I expect things to pick up as the weather gets warmer. How about you?" Clint sipped his coffee, then split the pastry in half.

"It's the usual for February," Oliver said. "But I got a strange call from Grace Porter a little while ago."

"Something wrong at the inn?"

Oliver shrugged. "You remember that big old tree that got hit by lightning several years ago?"

Clint lowered his eyes. He'd never forget. When the climbing tree split in two, so had his heart. All over again. "I remember."

"Did you ever go out to see what Austin Price designed?" Oliver asked.

"Never made the time."

Instead, Clint had gone out there before the work was done—the very afternoon that Oliver called to see if he wanted to bid on the project. Early one evening, when dusk settled on the lake, he rowed his boat to a sandy bar on the property west of the inn and made his way to the remains of the climbing tree. He'd sat on the damaged trunk, head bent, as he relived their childhood memories. His and Presley's.

Memories of every summer together had scrolled through his mind, one after the other. As if he were watching a film, he saw them change from rambunctious ten-year-olds to ambitious teens looking forward to the future. Then, suddenly, it was their last summer. The one after they both graduated from high school. He'd worked the breakfast shift at the diner as a busboy and done odd jobs for whoever needed something done. "No job too small or too hard" had been his motto.

Out there at the climbing tree, Clint had allowed himself to remember the day he and Presley buried the memory box. The tender moment when he'd gathered the courage to kiss her for the first time. He'd dug her photo from his wallet and stared again into the gorgeous brown eyes that always seemed to see into his soul.

But he couldn't let himself relive that last day. The day Presley left without a word. No letter. No message. Nothing.

Before the sting behind his eyes had become tears, Clint had dug up the memory box, stuck her photo inside, and closed it.

He'd never gone back to the climbing tree again.

"You okay?" Oliver asked.

"Sorry." Clint forced a smile. "You were saying something about that tree?"

"Not so much the tree as the dirt around it. Grace said someone has been digging holes in it." Oliver shook his head. "It's the strangest thing."

Clint narrowed his eyes. "Digging holes? Why?" A strange sensation flooded his stomach.

"I would have guessed it was kids with nothing better to do. Except . . ." Oliver sat back in his seat as Angel arrived with his coffee and a fudge brownie.

Clint handed her the bill. "This cover it?"

"And then some," Angel said. "I'll be right back with your change."

"Keep it," Clint said.

"Thank you." Angel smiled and bustled away.

Oliver bit into his brownie. "That's good. I'd eat one of these every day if my wife wasn't so bent on watching my waistline." He grinned. "You won't tell her about this, will you?"

"You can count on me." Clint tapped his finger against the side of his cup. "Except?"

"Except what?" Oliver asked.

"You said something about kids digging those holes. Except?"

"Oh, that. I had visitors at the shop this morning. One of them was Trent Jacobs. Can you believe it?"

"The football player?" Clint asked.

"That's right. Got my picture taken with him. I'll show you." Oliver wiped his hands on a napkin, then dug his phone out of his pocket and tapped the screen a few times. He proudly turned his phone around so Clint could see the photo.

Clint took the phone and examined the picture. It was Trent Jacobs all right. But what did he have to do with the climbing tree?

"Got his autograph too," Oliver said. "He's a real nice guy."

"Too nice to dig holes in someone else's garden?" Clint asked.

Oliver laughed. "Probably. I'm sure it wasn't him. Just strange that he wanted to know who had designed the garden. Seems to me that means he must have seen it."

"I don't understand." A tropical storm seemed to have taken hold inside Clint, making it impossible for him to hold on to any single thought. It was too much. Talking about the climbing tree. Trying not to remember the pain of Presley's unexplained departure. "Why is Trent Jacobs even in town?"

"I don't know, but he's staying at the Magnolia Harbor Inn." Oliver took the last bite of his brownie and washed it down with a gulp of coffee. "It's odd, don't you think? First, he comes asking about the landscape designer. Then Grace calls about those holes. It must be a coincidence."

Clint nodded.

"He said he wasn't moving down this way," Oliver continued. "But I can't help but feel he was being a bit cagey. You know, not wanting everyone to find out about his personal business. Maybe he wants to hire that same designer."

"Maybe so." Clint picked his pastry into pieces. He no longer had an appetite. Thoughts of Presley seemed to do that to him.

"I told him about you too," Oliver said. "If I hear he's ready to hire someone, I'll be sure and put in another good word for you."

"Thanks. I appreciate it." Clint downed the rest of his coffee and peered through the window. Where was Glen? Probably held up by a parishioner.

"Guess I'd better be going." Oliver gathered his trash and stood. "Thanks for paying."

"Anytime."

Oliver hesitated. "There was something about that woman. She looked kind of familiar."

The tropical storm stopped blowing—as if Clint had entered its calm eye. All was still. Too still. "What woman?"

"An attractive woman was with Trent. They made a nice couple."

The bell on the door jingled.

But Clint barely heard it. "Do you know her name?"

"Let me think a minute." Oliver scratched his head. "Something King, I think."

The storm circled again, swirling and thrashing. Had he really expected the woman to be Presley? Why would she be here now?

"So sorry I'm late." Glen rushed up to the table, his arm clasped around a bulging notebook. "Hello there, Oliver. Good to see you. Did Clint tell you what I'm getting Penny for Valentine's Day?"

Clint slowly pushed back his chair. While the two men talked, he got up and headed to the counter.

Angel graced him with a sympathetic smile. "You look like you need more coffee."

"Yes, please." What he needed was a new heart. One that hadn't been pummeled nearly ten years ago by hurricane-force winds.

It was strange. He hadn't felt this bad when Margot handed him back her engagement ring.

Presley

"I guess we should have gotten here earlier," Presley said as Trent bought the movie tickets. "I never guessed it would be so crowded. Especially on a Wednesday night."

"That's why." Trent pointed to a poster on the door as they entered the theater. "It's Palentine's Night."

"Clever marketing strategy." She gazed around the interior. The lobby had been renovated, but it still maintained its vintage charm. The mouthwatering aroma of popcorn filled the air as did the murmur of cheerful voices.

Had the entire town decided to see a movie tonight? Would Clint be here?

Presley closed her eyes and silently reprimanded herself. She had to stop hoping for and dreading the idea of running into him. The town wasn't that small. The likelihood of their paths crossing was slim to none.

Especially when she was determined it wouldn't happen.

"Do you want a hot dog and a soda?" Trent asked.

"Sure," she said. "Thanks."

When it was their turn to order, she scanned the crowd. A few people had noticed Trent, but they seemed to be doing their best not to stare at him. Presley smiled to herself and shifted her gaze.

Her heart stopped beating, and she froze.

Clint was here. In this theater.

"You okay?" Trent asked.

She nodded, not trusting herself to speak.

"He's here, isn't he?"

Presley nodded again.

Trent glanced around, even though he didn't know what Clint looked like, then leaned closer to Presley. "Do you want to leave?"

She raised her eyes to his and was undone by the compassion she saw there.

The clerk set the sodas on the counter beside three hot dogs and a tub of popcorn. He read off the amount on the cash register.

Trent handed the clerk a credit card, but his focus remained on Presley.

"It's fine," she said. Trent had insisted on buying the tickets and now all this food. It wouldn't be right to ask him to leave. "Let's go find our seats."

"Are you sure?" Trent asked.

"Yes." She stuffed a handful of napkins into her purse, then grabbed the hot dogs.

Trent juggled the popcorn and sodas.

As they walked, Presley resisted the urge to turn around and get a better glimpse of Clint. In that unexpected glance, brief as it was, her brain had imprinted the image of his profile. His jaw appeared more angular beneath the scruff of a day-old beard, and small lines appeared at the edges of his eyes that hadn't been there before. But she hadn't been mistaken. It was definitely him.

He'd been looking down, laughing at something. But she turned away before she saw who was with him. Who else could it be except the love of his life?

Another reason not to look.

She preceded Trent into the dim auditorium. The previews hadn't started yet, but a promotional program showed a behind-the-scenes peek at an upcoming film. By the time they'd found their seats, a soft drink ad was on the screen.

Presley exchanged Trent's two hot dogs for her soda and stuck the cup in the holder.

"What if he sees you?" Trent asked. "We can still go."

"With all this food?"

"It's paid for," Trent said. "We could find a place to park. Count the cars that go by. Play the license plate game."

Presley squelched a giggle. "You really want to do that?"

"No." His tone turned serious. "But I don't want you miserable during the entire movie either."

"I won't be," she assured him.

Trent held out his pinkie finger. "Promise?"

She hooked her little finger around his. "I promise."

The theater lights dimmed, and the crowd quieted.

After all, what did it matter if Clint saw her? What would he see? Though she and Trent weren't exactly on a date, Clint wouldn't know that. He'd see her with an attractive and attentive guy, a guy other people noticed and recognized. When they'd taken their seats, the murmuring had grown and heads had turned their way.

She and Clint could say hello like two mature adults. She could introduce Trent, and Clint could introduce her to his wife. And then they'd go their separate ways. Simple as that.

But Presley knew it would never be that simple.

Clint

"This counts as supper," Clint told Donnie when they got in the crowded concession line. The theater's Palentine's event was certainly a success. "Do you want a hot dog or a slice of pizza?"

Donnie stared at the menu board. For most people, the decision would be an easy one. But Donnie had to take his time. He needed to see the words and sound them out, recognizing each option before choosing one.

"You can have both if you want," Clint said.

Donnie's gaze jerked toward him, and his face lit up as if Christmas had come ten months early. "You mean it?"

"Why not?" Clint grinned. "It's my Palentine's treat to you."

"Okay." Donnie stressed each syllable of the simple word. He appeared thoughtful. "I want to give you a Palentine's treat too."

"Your being here is treat enough for me," Clint told his brother. "I missed you while you were gone."

"I didn't miss anybody." Donnie's eyes grew bright.

Clint prepared himself to hear one more time about all the new friends his brother had made on the trip and the activities he'd participated in. His voice, childish in its enthusiasm yet deep as any man's, wrapped Clint in a comforting bubble.

When he'd picked Donnie up at Hope Shelter, he'd run into the owner of the bakery that Margot had selected. Clint and Margot had met with the baker shortly after their engagement to secure a wedding cake. Margot was convinced every bride within a hundred-mile radius of Magnolia Harbor was planning a Valentine's Day wedding, and she was adamant about taking care of details as soon as possible.

The owner, who was dropping off cupcakes for someone's birthday, didn't say anything to Clint about the canceled order. She didn't need to. The pity in her eyes said it all. They'd exchanged the usual pleasantries, and she went on her way.

As Donnie told Clint—for the fourth time—about the bus ride home, Clint tried to shake off the uneasiness that had been unsettling him since yesterday. He supposed seeing the baker had brought back all the feelings of embarrassment, the distaste of being the object of everyone's pity.

They needn't bother.

He was fine. Being here with Donnie was exactly where he wanted to be. The breakup had been a good thing. But Clint couldn't say that to the people in this town. They just didn't want to believe him.

Donnie laughed as he repeated a joke the bus driver had told them.

Clint laughed too, but then a shiver washed over him. What had just happened?

"Hey, look." The guy standing in front of them spoke in a low voice to his buddy. "Isn't that Trent Jacobs?"

"Where?" his friend asked, glancing around.

Clint followed his gaze.

"Up there. Paying for his food."

"That can't be him. What would Trent Jacobs be doing here?"

"It looks like him."

That's because it is *him.* Clint decided not to tell the teen that he was right. Word would get around soon enough, and the football star might want to enjoy a movie without being swarmed by fans.

Especially when he was with—

Clint's heart stopped as the slender brunette who was with him grabbed a handful of napkins from the dispenser. One, two, three pulls.

Just like she had every single time they'd ever gone to a movie.

Presley.

Clint turned his head in the other direction. His heart fell like a stone to his feet. What could she possibly be doing here?

He thought back to his conversation with Oliver. *An attractive woman was with Trent. They made a nice couple.*

But why did Oliver think her last name was King? That didn't make any sense.

Clint's stomach lurched again. The holes at the climbing tree. The football star wouldn't have a reason for digging those holes, but maybe Presley did.

The line moved forward, and Clint adjusted his position while trying to pay attention to Donnie's story. He wanted to see Presley again—to prove to himself that his eyes hadn't betrayed him—but he didn't want her to see him. He bent his head toward Donnie but shifted his gaze toward the front of the concession stand.

Presley and Trent walked past the glass counters to the ticket taker, whose eyes widened and shoulders straightened. He exchanged a few words with the football star while Presley watched with a broad smile on her face.

Was it just him, or did that smile not quite reach her eyes?

Clint couldn't stop himself from gazing around the seats when he and Donnie entered the auditorium. The old movie house had been renovated more than once over the years. It now had three screens instead of one, so there was only a one-in-three chance that Presley and her date were seeing the same movie as he and Donnie.

The entryway of this particular auditorium was near the rear. A few upper rows were to their left, but most of the rows and the screen were to their right. As usual, Donnie headed toward the top row.

Clint hoped those one-in-three odds were with him while also hoping they weren't. He wanted to see Presley, maybe even talk to her. But what did they really have to say to each other after all this time? They'd been kids when she left. Recent high school graduates with their whole lives ahead of them.

As much as he hated to admit it, her abrupt departure was probably the best thing for both of them. They'd been too young to hold each other to promises of forever love.

But the ache of her disappearance, especially without a final goodbye, still hurt.

Clint settled into the seat beside Donnie and helped his brother organize his food. He squirted ketchup and relish on his own hot dog and scanned the rows below.

There they were—about halfway down the auditorium, engaging in what appeared to be a quiet but serious conversation. Presley took a bite of her hot dog as she gazed at Trent Jacobs. He said something, laughed, and handed her a napkin. She wiped her mouth and chin.

Mustard. It had to have been mustard. How many times had Clint done the same?

The theater dimmed for the previews, and more people filed into the seats.

Someone had been digging holes in that garden. Had that someone been Presley?

Clint and Presley had promised to dig up the memory box

together in ten years. But the ten years wouldn't be over until August. Six months from now.

A niggling suspicion snaked its way into Clint's thoughts. Had Presley returned to get the box before the time was up?

But why would she do that?

Maybe because she was starting a life with someone new. Maybe she wanted to put the past behind her once and for all before she gave her heart to someone else. To Trent Jacobs.

Presley could dig all the holes she wanted. She'd never find the box. And he wouldn't let her have it even if she asked him for it.

The box was his now.

The box and its memories were his.

When the movie ended, Clint wanted to rush out of the auditorium, but it never did any good to rush Donnie. And Donnie liked to watch the credits to the very end. He'd loudly protest if Clint tried to make him leave before he was ready.

He'd just have to hope that Presley didn't glance their way when she left the theater.

He needn't have worried. The couple gathered their belongings and walked out with most of the crowd. Presley seemed to keep her attention straight ahead or on Trent. It was almost as if she didn't want to see anyone else in the theater.

It didn't hurt that a few moviegoers recognized Trent. He chatted with a couple of teens while keeping one hand firmly on Presley's back.

Clint wanted to be glad for them. But it wasn't easy when he was feeling so sorry for himself.

Winnie

When Winnie breezed into the inn's kitchen after her morning walk, she found Grace loading the dishwasher.

As soon as Grace saw her, she hurried to her side. "Do you have any ideas about how to get Charlotte and Dean together?" she whispered.

"Where is Charlotte?" Winnie asked.

"Talking to Bethany and Joy. They're both interested in her cookbooks." Grace glanced at the door. "She may come in at any minute. Please tell me you have a plan."

"I have the idea for one—"

Grace practically squealed, then covered her mouth with her hand. "Sorry. I sounded like an excited fourteen-year-old."

"More like a ten-year-old," Winnie said with a gentle lilt in her voice. "The Busy Bees are meeting later this afternoon to work out the final details. Just leave everything to me."

"There's nothing you need me to do?"

"Not yet," Winnie said. "I'll let you know after our meeting."

"Thanks so much. I knew I could count on you." Grace's phone rang, and she checked the screen. "It's Oliver. Excuse me a minute."

Right after Grace went out one door of the kitchen, Charlotte entered from the other door. She noticed Winnie, then furtively glanced around. "Where's Grace?" she whispered.

"Hello to you too," Winnie said.

"I'm sorry." Charlotte enveloped her aunt in a hug. "I'm so anxious to talk to you without Grace overhearing us."

Winnie pointed to the other door. "She's on a phone call."

"Have you thought of any ideas for her and Spencer?" Charlotte asked.

"Maybe. The Busy Bees are meeting this afternoon, and we're going to finalize our plans." She held up her hands before Charlotte could ask any more questions. "I'll let you know what we decide as soon as I can."

Charlotte hugged her again. "Thank you. Spencer wants to make the day special for her. And I want it to be special for both of them."

"So do I, sweetheart," Winnie said. "So do I."

Charlotte glanced at the clock. "I hate to leave you like this, but I'm expecting a call from my publisher and I'm not quite prepared."

"Run along then," Winnie told her. "You don't need to worry about me."

"Thanks. I'll check in with you later."

A moment after Charlotte slipped out the rear door, Grace returned with Winston close behind. "Is Charlotte still in the dining room?"

"No, she just left. She's got a phone appointment with her publisher."

"Now?"

"Soon." Winnie studied her niece. "Is something wrong?"

"Oliver will be here in about ten minutes to check out the holes by the grandfather stump," Grace said. "But I have a meeting at the chamber of commerce, and I'm already running late. Could you go out there with him?"

Winnie frowned. "What holes?"

Grace's phone rang again. "Sorry. I need to get this. Can you stay?"

"There's nothing I'd rather do," Winnie said.

"Thanks. You're a dear." Grace rushed from the kitchen.

Winnie glanced at Winston. "Let's get to work." She appraised the kitchen, pushed up her sleeves, and finished loading the dishwasher.

Then she entered the dining room, cleared the table, added those dishes to the dishwasher, and finished tidying up both rooms.

As she dried her hands, a knock sounded from the rear door.

She found Oliver standing there. "Grace had to leave unexpectedly, so she asked me to go out to the grandfather stump with you. She was in such a hurry to leave that I'm afraid I don't understand what's going on."

"I don't either," Oliver replied. "She called me yesterday and said someone had dug holes where that oak tree got hit several years ago."

"Why would anyone be digging back there?" Winnie asked.

"No idea." Oliver craned his neck as if to see around her and into the house.

"What are you doing?" Winnie turned around to see if anyone was behind her. But only Winston sat there.

"Nothing." His ears reddened.

"Do you want a drink of water or a cup of coffee?" she asked.

"No, nothing like that," Oliver answered. "I just thought maybe, well, you know that Trent Jacobs stopped by my place yesterday. He said he was staying here."

"He is, but I haven't seen him today."

"Do you know what he's doing in town?" Oliver asked.

"Even if I did, I couldn't tell you," Winnie said. "We take the privacy of our guests very seriously."

"I didn't mean for you to break any confidences," he said. "I'm kind of hoping he plans to settle here. Wouldn't that put Magnolia Harbor on the map?"

"It certainly would for you sports lovers." Winnie took off her shoes and put on a pair of boots she kept at the back door for unexpected jaunts like this one. "Let's go check out those holes."

Winston led the way as they headed to the stump. When they reached it, the dog trotted around, sniffing.

"I don't understand," Winnie said, scanning the area. "Who would do something like this?"

"I don't know," Oliver said. "But the woman with Trent asked a lot of questions about this place. She wanted to know who'd done the work here."

A shiver went up Winnie's spine. There was only one woman Trent had spent much time with since coming to the inn.

"I think she said her name was King, but don't quote me on that."

"King?" Winnie shook her head. "Could it have been Presley Ingram?"

Oliver laughed. "That's it. Presley."

"How did you get 'King' out of that?" she asked.

"It's obvious, isn't it? Presley. Elvis Presley. The King."

Winnie laughed. "I suppose it is."

Oliver walked around the garden, then knelt down beside one of the holes. "Guess someone was searching for something. Come to think of it, Presley asked about a metal box. But I didn't find anything like that when I was out here."

A metal box? Winnie tightened her jacket against a sudden chill.

"This can easily be fixed up." Oliver stood and surveyed the area. "The place needs a bit of spring cleaning anyway."

"I'm sure Grace would be glad for you to take care of it," Winnie said.

"I can come over first thing next week if that's okay."

"Thanks. I'll let Grace know."

But first, Winnie had another mission to take care of. She needed to have a chat with Presley.

Presley

Presley slipped the trowel into her tote and headed toward the rear veranda. She needed to do something about the holes she'd dug and try to figure out what to do next. This was the perfect time. Trent had gone into town for another business meeting.

As she went out the door, she almost ran into Winnie.

"I'm so sorry," Presley said. The tote bag fell from her arm, and the tip of the trowel protruded from the opening.

"No harm done." Winnie picked up the tote before Presley could grab it. "I thought it must be you."

Heat flooded Presley's cheeks, but she forced what she hoped would appear to be an innocent smile. "What must be me?"

"Our mysterious digger." Winnie handed the tote to Presley. "I'm walking back to my house, and I wouldn't mind a bit of company."

"You're inviting me to your house?" Presley asked.

"I am."

"You're not mad at me?" Presley hated that her voice had taken on the tone of a scolded child. But she couldn't help it. She'd received tongue-lashings from her mother for smaller infractions. Something seemed strange about Winnie inviting her to her home after what Presley had done.

"I'm curious." Winnie shrugged. "This isn't the first time you've been at the inn, is it?"

Presley shook her head.

"Would you like to talk about it?" Winnie asked.

153

"I'm not sure."

"Let's take a walk," Winnie suggested. "It's a fine day for it."

Presley fell into step beside the older woman.

Winnie didn't pry. She allowed Presley time to put her scrambled thoughts into some kind of order.

"I suppose I owe you an explanation," Presley finally said. "Or maybe I owe it to Grace and Charlotte."

"You don't owe us anything," Winnie said.

"I was going back out there to fix the holes." Presley sighed. "I never meant to make so many."

"You didn't find what you wanted."

"It's gone." Presley waited for Winnie to ask her why she'd been digging and what she hoped to find.

But Winnie stayed silent, giving Presley more time with her thoughts.

"The mansion belonged to my grandparents," Presley said. "It had been in Grandma's family for generations."

Winnie nodded. "I didn't know your grandparents very well. Only that they were one of our older families."

"The property became too much for them, but they wouldn't sell it. I don't think they could imagine their family home belonging to anyone else."

"It must be hard for you," Winnie said. "Seeing it as an inn and belonging to my nieces."

"Yes. And no." Presley swiped at a stray tear. She wouldn't cry. Not now when there was no need to. Not when she had an audience. Mother would be horrified.

"What do you mean?" Winnie asked.

"I hoped it would be my home one day," Presley replied. "But life didn't work out that way. I'm glad it did for Grace and Charlotte. They love it here, and all their renovations are beautiful. My grandparents would love to have seen what they've done to the place."

"When were you last here?" Winnie asked.

"For the funeral. But Mother insisted we fly in and out again on the same day. It was like she didn't want me staying here any longer than necessary. I didn't even get to come out to the house, and she refused to include me in any of the decisions. I was able to get only a couple of heirlooms."

They stopped at the edge of Lake Haven Road. Though it was the main road leading to town, no cars were coming from either direction.

Presley took a deep breath, inhaling the soft scents invigorated by fresh lake water and sunshine-soaked breezes. How quiet it was out here, even though it was only a mile or so from the bustle of a quaint town.

"I could use a cup of tea to warm my bones," Winnie said. "Please say you'll join me."

"I'd like that." Presley followed Winnie across the road.

The two women walked in silence toward the Bennett home.

"I remember riding my bike past your house when I stayed with my grandparents," Presley said. "I wish now that I had stopped to say hello."

"Children have too many other things to keep them busy to bother with old folks." Winnie smiled. "I remember you too. Didn't you spend a lot of time with Clint Calloway?"

"We were good friends." Presley averted her gaze. "Back then."

"You're not now?" Winnie opened the back door and gestured for Presley to precede her into the bright utility room.

Instead of answering, Presley balanced herself against the washing machine and slipped off her shoes.

Winnie sat on a bench to remove her boots. "I usually keep these at the inn," she said with a chuckle. "But I forgot to get my shoes when we bumped into each other."

"I can take them back for you if you'd like," Presley offered.

"No need. I'll wear them tomorrow and exchange them." Winnie stood and removed her jacket. "Come on into the kitchen. I think I have a few homemade oatmeal cookies we can have with our tea."

"I'm going to go home with at least ten additional pounds," Presley said. "Not that I'm complaining. The food at the inn is amazing."

"It's one of the reasons we have so many returning guests." Winnie busied herself with boiling water and setting out a tea tray.

A tabby cat glided past her ankle. Presley reached down, and the cat meowed as she rubbed her head against Presley's palm. "Who's this?"

"Her name is Phoebe," Winnie replied. "Gus and I adopted her about six years ago from a rescue group."

"She's lovely." Presley knelt down and scratched Phoebe behind the ears. She was rewarded with a deep purr. "I'd like to have a pet. But I work long hours, and it wouldn't be fair to the animal."

"Your work must be exciting," Winnie commented, putting a few oatmeal cookies on a plate and adding it to the tray. "Surrounded by all that style and sophistication."

"The glamor is overrated." Presley straightened and rested her hands on the back of a kitchen chair. "It's gratifying to create designs that win awards and to have a few of the top models eager to work with me. But there's something that seems inauthentic about the whole thing. It's not like here."

"You could always come back." Winnie retrieved two teacups from a cabinet and set them on the tray. "Though I suppose that wouldn't be easy for you with your career. We don't have much demand for haute couture in Magnolia Harbor."

Presley hung her head. "I couldn't come back here anyway."

"Does that have anything to do with the reason for your digging?"

"We buried a memory box there," Presley said as she wiped away a stray tear. "The last summer I was here."

"You and Clint?" Winnie asked.

Presley nodded.

"You're searching for it." Winnie's gentle voice made it hard for Presley to hold back her tears.

She swallowed the growing lump in her throat and faced the older woman. "When I was in the eighth grade, I played Wendy in my school's production of *Peter Pan*. I told Clint all about it, and he surprised me by memorizing all of Peter's lines."

Winnie smiled at her with warm encouragement.

Presley smiled back, and her voice strengthened as she continued sharing the memory. "I'll never forget sitting as high up in the climbing tree as we dared to go and acting out our favorite scenes."

"The climbing tree?" Winnie echoed. "I'm guessing that's the grandfather tree that was hit by lightning."

"Yes, and I can't believe it's gone."

"I am sorry." The teakettle whistled, and Winnie poured the boiling water into a china teapot. She put the teapot on the tray with the cups and plate of cookies. "Let's go into the living room. The chairs are more comfortable in there."

Presley settled into a deep upholstered chair in front of a huge bay window with a view of Lake Haven Road. Across the road were a couple of houses, and beyond them was the lake. "You live in a beautiful home. And in a beautiful place."

Winnie set the tray on an end table. "Thank you. We love it here." She poured two cups of tea and handed one to Presley. "It's especially nice having Grace and Charlotte nearby."

"I envy that too."

Winnie raised an eyebrow as she sat down next to Presley. "What do you mean?"

"The relationship you have with them." Presley lowered her head so her hair formed a barrier between them. "I've hardly spoken to my mother since my grandparents died. And we have no other relatives."

"What about your father?" Winnie asked gently.

"He moved to New Mexico when I was still a toddler," Presley said. "He remarried and had more kids."

"I'm very sorry," Winnie said.

Presley shrugged and rubbed her arms. "I don't usually tell people that. Especially not when I first meet them."

"I'm glad you told me. I'd like to pray for you and your family if that's all right with you."

"I believe in prayer," Presley said. "But God has been answering 'no' on this one for a long time. I'm afraid it might be too late."

"It's never too late," Winnie said. "Tell me more about *Peter Pan*. It's been a long time since I've read it or seen it."

Presley took a moment to gather her thoughts. She'd already confided so much in Winnie. She might as well share the rest of the sad story. "Do you remember the part about the thimble? And the acorn?"

"I think I do. Wendy wanted to give Peter a kiss, but he didn't know what a kiss was. So Wendy gave him her thimble and told him it was a kiss."

"That's right," Presley said. "And he gave her an acorn button. It saved her life when an arrow shot by one of the lost boys hit the button instead of Wendy's heart."

"Why do I get the feeling a thimble and an acorn have something to do with your memory box?"

Presley gazed into her teacup. The fragrant aroma soothed the hurt caused by dredging up the memory. "When it was time for me to leave that summer, Clint gave me an acorn button, and I gave him a thimble. Every summer after that, we gave each other little gifts. Then, that last summer, after we'd both graduated from high school, we decided to put a few of our special tokens in a memory box."

"Which you buried near the climbing tree," Winnie said.

Presley nodded. "We promised not to open it for ten years."

"This is the tenth year?" Winnie asked, then took a sip of tea.

"In August," Presley said. "We were going to open the box together. But my mother believed that Clint was a summer fling and he was going to ruin my chances of a successful career."

"So that's why you haven't stayed in touch with him," Winnie said.

"Yes. My mother told me that Clint was engaged. So I came back for the box, but I can't find it. I don't know if Clint already dug it up or if someone else discovered it. All I know is that I wanted it. And now it's gone."

"You haven't talked to Clint, have you?"

"I saw him at the movie theater last night, but he didn't see me." Unable to sit a moment longer, Presley got to her feet and walked over to the window. A bicyclist came into view and stopped at the end of the drive. "I don't want him to know I'm in town. I just wish I could find out if he has the box."

The bicyclist removed his helmet and stared at the Bennett house.

Presley gasped as the man pedaled closer.

"But don't you know—"

"It's him," Presley said, interrupting Winnie. She pointed out the window. "He's coming here."

Winnie joined her and peered through the glass. "Clint."

"I can't let him find me here."

"Hold on a minute," Winnie said.

"No. I can't." Presley raced through the kitchen to the utility room and slid on her shoes.

Winnie followed. "Please stay and let me explain something to you."

"Thank you for listening and for the tea," Presley said, ignoring Winnie's plea. "For everything."

Before Winnie could say another word, Presley pushed through the back door and ran to the woods behind the house. She'd explored this area enough times in her youth to know how to return to the inn without being seen.

Clint would never even catch a glimpse of her.

24

Clint

Clint parked his bike in the grass near the sidewalk at Winnie's house and slid the helmet strap onto the handlebars. He pressed his hand against his abdomen, trying to steady himself, while deciding whether he should go through with this.

He'd hardly slept at all last night, and when he did, he dreamed of Presley. Images of her seemed to be everywhere. At the theater. At the coffee shop. At the bookstore. At the park. On the lake.

All the places where they'd hung out together on those long summer days. During their later teen years, she'd gone with him when he had odd gardening jobs, both of them getting their hands dirty as they pulled weeds and planted shrubs. Clint had always tried to split his pay with her, but she wouldn't allow it. A ticket to a movie or a milkshake from the ice cream parlor was all she ever wanted.

Presley hadn't made it seem like charity, though she knew he needed the money. Somehow they'd understood that working together, being together, was what they both wanted out of life. What they wanted in their future.

Until one day . . .

Clint shook away that memory, not wanting to revisit it.

Presley was back in Magnolia Harbor. He'd seen her at the theater last night. And he knew without a doubt that she'd been walking up the drive with Winnie when he pedaled by.

Stunned by seeing her, Clint had kept going, following the curve of the road toward town. But as he approached the downtown area, he'd made a U-turn.

Presley might not want to see him or talk to him. But she had to have been the one digging the holes at the climbing tree. He could tell her not to bother. That he already had the memory box and he planned to keep it.

After all, she was the one who walked away. Not him.

The pain from that day hit Clint in the chest with the power of a freight train. It also strengthened his resolve. Before he could change his mind, he hurried to the front door and knocked.

Winnie opened the door. "Won't you come in?"

Clint stepped inside and glanced around the comfortable living room. "Where is she?"

"Where's who?" she asked.

"Presley Ingram," he said. "I know she's here."

"She was, but she's gone now." Winnie took a seat and pointed to the other chair. "Please have a seat."

"Where did she go?" Clint asked. "I need to talk to her."

"Why don't you and I have a chat first?" Winnie asked. "I've already poured you a cup of tea."

"I mean no disrespect but—"

She held up a hand. "And I don't mean to be difficult. But there's a time and a place for all things. I don't know that this is the time for you to talk to Presley."

He held her gaze and released a heavy sigh. "She doesn't want to see me."

Winnie sat back in her chair. "Not right now."

"What did she tell you?" Clint asked as he finally sat down. Somehow the tightness in his chest seemed to ease. He picked up the full cup of tea and took a long sip of the hot liquid. He didn't care that much for the taste, but the warmth provided a kind of comfort he desperately needed.

"We talked about *Peter Pan*," Winnie said quietly. "And the memory box."

"She can't have it."

"You already dug it up." She nodded slowly. "I thought perhaps that was the case."

"After the climbing tree was hit," he said. "I didn't want anyone else to find it."

"If I remember right, Oliver Nichols recommended you as the designer for that garden," Winnie said. "I wondered at the time why you refused it. You were getting your business off the ground, and it would have been a good project for your portfolio. But now I understand."

"I knew the tree had to be destroyed after it was hit by lightning." Clint swallowed the growing lump in his throat. "But I couldn't work on the project."

"You and Presley were so close back then," she remarked. "What happened?"

"One day she was here. The next day she was gone." He frowned. "No note. No message. Nothing."

"You tried to contact her?"

Clint nodded. "But she changed her phone number and blocked me on social media. Not that I was ever much for that kind of thing anyway. I even wrote her several snail mail letters, but she didn't write back." He gripped the armrests of the chair. It seemed to take all his willpower to stay seated. "I got the message loud and clear."

"But are you sure you know who was sending that message?" Winnie asked.

He stared at her for a long moment. "What do you mean?"

"Perhaps someone who didn't want Presley's future career to be derailed by a summer fling."

"It wasn't a fling," Clint said. "Not to me."

Winnie remained silent.

Suddenly, all the puzzle pieces fell into place. He should have known. "Her mother."

Winnie peered out the window, as if she sought answers beyond the glass. "I'm sure Presley's mother thought she was doing what was best for her daughter. Don't judge her too harshly."

"Where is Presley now?" Clint asked. "I need to see her."

"She thinks you're married."

He gaped at her. "You didn't tell her I wasn't?"

"She saw you coming and rushed out before I could," Winnie explained.

"What am I supposed to do?" Clint asked, running his hand through his hair.

"Wait for the right time and the right place to talk to her," she said.

"You're talking in riddles, and I don't want to wait any longer."

"Please wait another day," Winnie said. "I think I can arrange the perfect time and place if you'll only be patient. I'll ask a few of my friends in The Busy Bees to help."

"What can you and your friends possibly do?" he asked.

"You might be surprised. Trust me."

Clint considered a moment, then nodded.

Tomorrow wouldn't be his wedding day, but maybe, God willing, it would be the day his true love returned.

25

Winnie

When The Busy Bees were seated around the table at Spool & Thread, Winnie stood before a whiteboard and wrote *Operation Romance* across the top in large red letters.

"Isn't this exciting?" Patty brushed her hair behind her shoulders. "We're actors in an unscripted play, my friends." Her green eyes widened. "No. We're the directors and the producers, taking care of all the details and making sure everything goes smoothly when the curtain rises."

"On an unscripted play," Helen said, "where the actors don't know their lines."

"Spencer will," Winnie said. "Let's start there."

"We're going to light a fire under those two," Patty said. "I do wish Angel was here. She could make a wooden heart engraved with their names and the date. What a wonderful keepsake that would be."

"Angel's working this afternoon," Judith said. "That's a great idea, though. Maybe someone could stop by the coffee shop after we've worked out the details and see if she has time to do something like that."

Helen raised her hand. "I will. I planned to stop in there anyway to get a bag of Caribbean roast. Keith has taken a liking to it."

"Thanks." Winnie turned back to the board and wrote *Timetable* on another section. "I thought we'd use the barn at the inn for our location. It shouldn't be hard to get Grace and Charlotte there at the right time."

"Tell them our plan," Judith said.

"Since Dean can't leave The Tidewater until late, we could arrange a dinner for Grace and Spencer first," Winnie said. "Judith and I worked out a timetable. Let me know what you think." She checked her notes.

Then she wrote on the board:

> *9:30 Spencer arrives*
>
> *9:45 Grace arrives*
>
> *11:30 Dean arrives*
>
> *11:45 Charlotte arrives*

"Spencer knows why he's there," Judith said. "But Winnie will tell Grace to be at the barn for Charlotte's surprise."

"But Grace will find Spencer there instead of Charlotte." Patty clasped her hands together, and her bracelets clinked. "How romantic."

"Charlotte will think she's going to the barn to sing for Grace and Spencer," Winnie added.

"And she'll find Dean." Patty practically swooned.

"How will you get Dean there?" Helen asked.

"We're asking him to bring dessert for Grace and Spencer," Judith said. "If everyone follows the timetable, it should work. Now let's talk about decorations and menus."

Winnie wrote the ideas on the whiteboard. Patty and Judith volunteered to take care of decorations, and the other women planned the menus.

When everyone had their assignments, Helen put away her pen

and notebook. "I'd better get going so I can talk to Angel."

"Could you wait a few more minutes?" Winnie asked. "I can't thank each of you enough for what you're doing for my nieces to make this a special Valentine's Day for them. I know it's asking a lot, but could we plan one more mission under Operation Romance?"

"Why?" Judith asked.

Winnie turned to the board, made her third bullet point, and wrote *Mission Reignite*.

Patty tilted her head. "Who are we reuniting?"

"Clint Calloway and—"

"Is Margot back?" Patty asked.

"Do you think that's wise?" Helen blurted out.

"No, ladies." Winnie held out her hands in a calm-down gesture. "I want to reunite Clint with someone else."

"Presley Ingram," Judith said.

"Who's Presley Ingram?" Patty asked.

"Her grandparents owned the mansion before Grace and Charlotte bought it," Winnie replied. "She spent summers here as a child."

"I remember her," Helen said. "She came to the house once with Clint when Keith hired him to do a few odd jobs around the house. She was such a sweet girl."

"Apparently, she and Clint spent most of their free time together when she was here," Winnie said. "And their friendship became something more."

"Then why aren't they married?" Patty asked.

"Presley's mother." Winnie explained to the women what she'd learned in her conversations with Presley and Clint. "They still have feelings for each other. Perhaps not what they once had, but neither can truly move forward until they've at least resolved what happened in the past."

"Let's set up a romantic dinner for them too," Helen said. "Can you get them to the barn around seven? Then we'd have time to clear things away and prepare for Grace and Spencer."

"Not the barn," Winnie said. "I have something else in mind for them."

Grace

Only one apple cider doughnut remained from breakfast, so Grace put it on a small plate and poured herself another cup of coffee. "I'll do the dishes after I finish this," she said to Charlotte. "We need to have these doughnuts on the menu again."

Winston, who was napping on the floor, raised his head and yipped as if in agreement.

The sisters laughed.

"I'm glad the guests liked them." Charlotte glanced at the plates piled on the counter. "Are you sure you don't want my help?"

"Positive. You're still working on galleys, aren't you?"

"I am, but I have another week before they're due back to the publisher. I don't want to leave you with a mess."

"You're not," Grace assured her. "It won't take long to clean up. And all our guests have plans this morning, so I can quickly refresh the rooms."

"What about Presley and Trent?" Charlotte's eyes sparkled with mischief. "Do they have the same plans?"

"I saw them walking to the parking lot." Grace shrugged. "But they both have rental cars, so I don't know if they left together or not."

"I'll check on my way to the cottage," Charlotte said. "Leave the laundry for me. I'll do it this afternoon."

"Deal." Grace perched on one of the island stools and bit into the tasty doughnut. Though Grace was a good cook in her own right, Charlotte was a genius. Of course, she'd been trained, but even as a teenager, she'd been creative in the kitchen.

"See you later," Charlotte said as she headed out the door.

Grace waved goodbye and sighed when the door closed behind her sister. She'd awakened with a definite case of the blues. Today was Valentine's Day. She hadn't seen Spencer since Tuesday, and then he'd been more interested in talking football with Trent than anything else.

She really hadn't expected anything from him. But she couldn't help feeling a little disappointed—okay, a lot disappointed—that he hadn't suggested dinner. She'd have even been content with lunch.

In this day and age, she could have asked him. But that was not how she wanted their story to be. If they ever had a story.

The door opened, and Winnie walked in. "Good morning."

Winston jumped up and bounded over to Winnie. He wagged his tail.

She bent down to pet him, then turned to Grace. "That doughnut looks good."

"It's another of Charlotte's fabulous creations," Grace said. "You want a taste?"

Winnie sampled the donut. "Very good."

Grace glanced around to be sure Charlotte hadn't returned. "Today's the day. Did The Busy Bees come up with a plan to surprise Charlotte?"

Her aunt nodded.

"I'm so glad. Tell me."

"Judith and Patty will be over later to decorate the barn. It would be best if you stayed away until this evening."

"Don't they want my help?" Grace asked.

"No," Winnie said. "They have all the help they need."

Grace raised her eyebrows. "You're acting secretive."

"We don't want Charlotte to get suspicious," Winnie explained. "She might go searching for you and find you in the barn."

"Then what can I do?" Grace asked.

"We're preparing a lovely and intimate romantic dinner for them," her aunt assured her. "All you need to do is show up at 9:45 this evening looking lovely."

"Why do I have to look lovely?"

"Because you're going to be the hostess," Winnie answered. "And you can take photos too." She tilted her head. "Unless you have other plans. I'm sorry. I shouldn't have assumed . . ."

"No, I don't have any plans," Grace said. "Tonight I'm living vicariously through my sister."

Winnie patted her hand. "Sometimes that's all we can do. Speaking of Charlotte, where is she?"

"I sent her home to work on her book."

"Do you need a hand with the dishes or the rooms?" Winnie offered.

"No thanks," Grace said. "I'll get everything done."

"Nonsense. You go tidy up the rooms, and I'll take care of the kitchen." Winnie smiled. "Consider it my Valentine's Day gift to you."

Grace hesitated, then agreed. At least she was getting one Valentine's Day gift this year. She mentally shook her head. No way was she going to spend the day feeling sorry for herself. That was not who she was, and it certainly wasn't who she wanted to be.

Grace enveloped her aunt in a warm embrace. "Thank you for helping me with the surprise for Charlotte. And thank The Busy Bees too. This means a lot."

Winnie smiled. "Anything for my girls."

27

Winnie

As soon as the dishes were finished, Winnie walked to the cottage to see Charlotte. She found her niece curled up in a corner of her sofa with a stack of pages in her lap.

"The new cookbook?" Winnie asked.

"Yes." Charlotte patted the seat beside her. "Come and see. The galleys show black-and-white photos, but even so, it's obvious they'll be gorgeous."

"Your publisher always does such a great job," Winnie said as she sat beside her. After the morning walk to the inn and helping Grace in the kitchen, she appreciated a few moments to get off her feet.

"Sometimes I still have to pinch myself," Charlotte continued. "Can you believe I actually get to do this?"

"Who else could do it better?"

"That's one of the things I love about you." Charlotte's warm smile lit up her face. "You'd love my cookbook even if all the recipes tasted awful."

"That's what aunts are for. Though in this instance, the praise is well deserved." Winnie tapped the stack of pages. "God gave you a special talent and the desire to share your creations with others. Your cookbooks are a blessing."

"That's a sweet thing for you to say," Charlotte responded. "I don't always think of them like that."

"How do you think of them?" Winnie asked.

"A joy. Sometimes a burden when the deadline is looming and my creativity seems to be gone."

"But you always come through." Winnie always said extra prayers for her niece during her crunch times. Prayers for calm and inspiration. God had never failed to answer those prayers. "You've never missed a deadline, and each cookbook is better than the last. You come up with so many wonderful new ideas each time."

"I suppose it's because of what you said earlier. It's something God gave me. And I don't ever want to take it for granted."

"I don't believe you ever will," Winnie said. "Now show me what's in store for your fans."

As they leafed through the galley pages together, Charlotte talked about the inspiration behind several of the recipes, and Winnie exclaimed over the photographs. Charlotte herself had taken several of them, setting up shots in the inn's kitchen, the dining room, the veranda, and even on the dock.

When the clock struck the quarter hour, Winnie started and checked the time. "I can't stay much longer. I actually stopped by to talk to you about Spencer."

"He called me last night, and I told him that you had everything planned. I think he's anxious." Charlotte placed the galley pages on the coffee table, then leaned back against the sofa cushions. "Isn't it romantic how he wants to make everything perfect for Grace? I don't care what she says. Sunday night's trip to see *Les Misérables* was definitely a date."

"I think you're right about that," Winnie said. "I talked to him earlier today, and everything is set. The Busy Bees are taking care of the food and decorations."

"Don't you want me to fix anything?" Charlotte asked. "I don't mind."

"Not this time." Winnie smiled, hoping Charlotte wouldn't press the issue. The plan had to work, but juggling all the moving parts sure wasn't easy. "Just be at the barn at 11:45."

Charlotte stared at her. "Why so late?"

"Didn't I tell you?" No, she probably hadn't. Not with so many other details on her mind. "You're the after-dinner entertainment. We couldn't think of anyone more talented than you to set a romantic mood by singing a few of their favorite songs."

"Don't you think I'll be in the way?" Charlotte asked. "You know, third wheel and all that?"

"It's too late to back out now," Winnie said. "The Busy Bees have already got the evening planned. After your set, you can suggest they go for a moonlit walk. Then we'll swoop in and clean up."

"I can help you with that too."

Oh no, you can't. But Winnie couldn't say anything about Dean showing up. "Help is always appreciated. Now I need to run. Good luck with the galleys."

As soon as Winnie closed the door behind her, she leaned against it and closed her eyes. All these little white lies were going to add up to one huge whopper before the night was over. And she wasn't even done yet.

She returned to the inn's lobby and logged into the computer. After tapping a few keys, she found what she needed—Trent Jacobs's phone number. She started to call him when he came sauntering in through the front door.

"Is Presley with you?" Winnie asked, looking behind him.

"I think she's hiding out in her room," Trent answered.

Winnie glanced toward the stairs, making sure Presley wasn't around. "I was about to call you. Could you do a little favor for me?"

"Need a few tips on how to intercept a pass?" he asked.

She searched his face for any sign of teasing, but his expression appeared serious. "No. Nothing like that."

A mischievous glint appeared in his eyes, and Trent chuckled.

"Sorry about that. But you remind me so much of my grandmother, and that's what I always say to her when she asks me for a favor. Then she pretends to get mad and gives me a swat."

Winnie smiled. "Your grandma sounds like a good sport."

"She's the best. And I do whatever she asks me to do." He folded his arms on the counter and leaned forward. "Now tell me about that favor."

"Let's go into the music room. I don't want anyone to overhear us." As Winnie led the way, her stomach clenched. The idea had seemed like a good one when she and her friends had discussed it. But until now she hadn't considered Trent's feelings. What if he cared about Presley? If so, how could she ask him to assist them with their plan?

Once they were seated in the upholstered chairs, Trent crossed his ankle over his knee.

Winnie folded her hands while trying to decide the best way to broach the subject.

"This must be something serious," he said.

"Yes." Winnie breathed a silent prayer. "Matters of the heart usually are."

"Whose heart?" Trent asked.

"Presley's. And someone else's. One of our local men."

"You mean Clint?"

"You know about him?" Winnie asked, surprised.

He nodded. "Presley's here because of him. Though she doesn't want him to know she's here."

"She told me that too."

"She said he's engaged or maybe married. Which is it?"

"Neither." Winnie flattened her palms and smoothed out a nonexistent wrinkle in her pants. "I talked to Presley yesterday, but she left before I could tell her the wedding was called off. It was supposed to be today."

"Wow. Poor guy."

Winnie studied the football player with fresh eyes, pleased by his sensitivity. Trent seemed like an upstanding and responsible man, someone who appreciated family and had good values. Winnie knew that she could trust his discretion.

"The breakup was mutual," she said, "and they remain friends. As much as people can be friends under such circumstances. Margot is in California now."

"I need to tell Presley." Trent started to rise.

But Winnie held up her hand to stop him. "Clint came by my house yesterday. He saw Presley at the movies."

"Did he now?" He settled back in his seat. "We saw him too."

"I'm not surprised. It's a small theater." Winnie couldn't help thinking that Clint and Donnie might not have been at the movies if she hadn't given them the tickets. *God works in mysterious ways.*

"Anyway, he seems hurt that she's been here all this time but hasn't gotten in touch with him," Winnie continued. "I'm wondering if you could help me get them together." She hesitated, then looked steadily into Trent's eyes. "Unless that would be hurting your heart?"

A slow smile lifted the corners of Trent's mouth. "You're a kindhearted person to think of me. And Presley's great. But I'm like the big brother she never had. And to me? Well, she's one more little sister. We definitely have a connection, but it's familial, not romantic."

Relief lifted a weight from Winnie's shoulders. "Then let me tell you about Mission Reignite."

After talking with Trent, Winnie headed for home. Along the way, she called Clint and asked him to meet her at the Dragonfly Coffee Shop in twenty minutes.

"Is this about Presley?" he asked.

"I'll explain everything when I see you," Winnie said. "Will you be there?"

"Of course," Clint said, but he didn't sound too enthusiastic.

Winnie wasn't sure what she had expected—more excitement surely. But it seemed Clint didn't know what to think or feel about Presley's return. Hopefully by the time the night was over, their heartaches would be healed.

She said goodbye to Clint, then called Judith. Winnie explained what she needed, and Judith promised to have the item ready for her to pick up at Spool & Thread before she met Clint.

In less than twenty minutes, Winnie entered the Dragonfly.

Angel greeted her. The woman's long dark hair was pulled back into a complicated braid adorned with red ribbons. Henna hearts decorated her olive skin. She pointed toward Clint, who was seated at a table near the window. "He already paid for your order. Do you want your usual?"

"That sounds fine," Winnie said. "Thank you."

Angel leaned over the counter and whispered, "Does he know about the mission?"

"I'm going to tell him now." Winnie crossed her fingers. "Let's hope he accepts it."

"I think he will." Angel grabbed a cup and wrote Winnie's name on the side. "Yesterday I saw Presley with Trent Jacobs. She's very chic."

"And very sweet." As soon as her order was ready, Winnie joined Clint and took her seat. "Thanks for the coffee."

He raised his own cup as if in a toast. "Consider it a Valentine's Day present from a friend."

"That's kind of you." She retrieved a small sack emblazoned with the Spool & Thread logo from her purse. "I have a Valentine's Day gift for you too."

"What is it?" Clint leaned back in his chair as if afraid of what he was going to find in the sack.

Winnie laughed at him and pushed the sack across the table. "Just open it."

Clint reached for the sack and peered inside. He grinned as he held up the contents. "A thimble? I garden, but I don't sew."

"It's not that kind of thimble," Winnie said.

"Then what kind of thimble is it?"

Winnie didn't answer as she held his gaze, willing him to understand.

A moment later, Clint averted his eyes and tapped the bottom of the thimble on the table. "Peter Pan's kiss."

"You remember."

"Did Presley give you this?" His voice was gruff as if he found the question difficult to ask. Saying Presley's name seemed especially hard for him.

If he'd been her son, Winnie would have pulled him into a motherly hug right there in the coffee shop. Though perhaps men didn't appreciate motherly hugs in public even when their hearts were obviously broken. She and Gus had been blessed with four lovely daughters but no boys.

"No, but I've been told she gave you one before," Winnie said in a soothing tone. "I thought you might want to return the favor."

"That was a long time ago," he said. "We were just kids."

"And now you're adults. Both single." Winnie paused and took a deep breath. The line between comforting and meddling was thinner than a needle point. She didn't want to cross it. But Clint and Presley needed to talk to each other. What happened after that was in their hands. And God's. "And I think both of you regret what happened in the past."

Clint tapped the thimble again, harder this time, and gazed out the window.

Winnie took a sip of her coffee. He needed silence, and there was nothing else for her to say. At least not yet.

Clint turned to Winnie. "She doesn't want to see me. If she did, she'd have . . ." He let his voice trail off, then gulped his drink.

Winnie wanted to tell him that she understood, but she didn't believe those were the words he needed to hear. She waited for him to speak.

He held up the thimble. "What am I supposed to do with this?" he finally asked.

"You may think that my friends and I are pushing our noses where they don't belong," she began.

Clint didn't respond. Another man might have walked out or said something smart in reply. But Clint was too good a person to say anything rude. Though that didn't mean he wasn't biting his tongue to keep from doing so.

"It's true," Winnie conceded. "We are. But only because we care about you. And because it's Valentine's Day. If there's any day in the entire year to take a chance on love, isn't it today?"

"I don't think you heard me," he said. "Presley is avoiding me."

"Maybe. Probably. But perhaps she has a reason for not seeing you."

"She's the one who left. Not me."

There was so much Winnie wanted to tell him. She had to bite her own tongue to keep the words from coming out. But her interference could only go so far. "Do you have plans for this evening?"

"I had expected to be at my wedding reception," Clint answered. "But as you and everyone else in this town knows, that's not happening."

"Then perhaps you'd be willing to take that thimble to the grandfather stump at the inn," she said. "I think you used to call it the climbing tree."

He studied her, his eyes clouded with something close to suspicion and doubt. "Why would I do that?"

"Someone else may be there."

Clint shook his head and leaned across the table. "Why are you and your friends trying to play matchmaker? You can't fix this."

"We're not trying to fix it," Winnie said. "We just want to give you a chance to talk to each other."

"Did Presley agree to this?" he asked.

Winnie shifted in her seat and needlessly stirred her coffee.

Clint fixed her with a knowing gaze. "She doesn't know." His words were flat.

"No, but she will be there." Winnie decided to play her last card. "She wants the memory box. That's why she's here. She's been searching for it. Digging holes around the stump that Oliver is going to have to fix."

"She can't have it," he said.

"It sounds to me like the box is special to both of you. Maybe it's time you took a look at it together."

Clint didn't say anything.

"When Presley's mother took her away almost ten years ago, there was nothing you could do to stop her interference," Winnie said. "There's nothing any of us can do to change what's happened in the past. But don't you see that now—today—you have a choice? You can let Presley leave town without talking to her. Or you can meet her at the place that means something special to both of you. You can talk about the fun times you had every summer. And maybe, just maybe, you'll get the chance to say whatever is in your heart before Presley leaves this time."

Clint watched her, his expression unreadable.

Winnie sat back in her seat. "Or you can be stubborn and go home and spend the evening in front to the TV or the computer or whatever you planned to do tonight to sulk."

"I wasn't going to sulk," Clint argued.

Winnie stood. "Remember that it's your choice." She picked up her cup and left the shop. It took every bit of willpower she had not to glance back. But she'd said her piece.

The ball was in Clint's court, as Trent might say.

No, that wasn't right. Trent played football, not basketball.

What would a football player say? She'd have to ask Gus.

Winnie had almost reached her car when someone shouted her name. She turned to see Clint jogging toward her.

When he reached her, he stopped and took a deep breath. "Are you sure she'll be there?"

"I talked to Trent," Winnie replied. "He'll see that she's there."

"Trent Jacobs? The football player?" Clint raised his eyes to the heavens as if imploring divine help. "That's who she was with at the movies."

"They're not dating," she told him. "There's nothing romantic between them."

"Are you sure?"

"Where is your good sense?" Winnie asked. She didn't mean to sound perturbed, but why couldn't he see what was so obvious? "Would Trent be in on the plan if he had any romantic interest in Presley? He told me himself that he thinks of her as a little sister."

"Then the man must be blind," Clint said. He shifted his weight from one foot to the other, then finally focused his gaze on Winnie. "What time should I be there?"

"At seven."

He pressed his lips together and nodded slowly. "Okay."

Winnie's shoulders relaxed. She hadn't even realized how tense she was. Her excitement bubbled into a quick rush of words. "You won't be sorry. And you don't have to worry about a thing. We have it all planned. We'll have food and drinks. And I'm going home right now to make a pie for dessert. Any kind you want."

"Any kind?" Clint seemed more relaxed now too. A smile tugged at the corner of his lips. "French silk is my favorite."

"I'll make one for you," she promised.

"I'll see you this evening." Clint shifted and nodded again. "At what's left of the climbing tree." He returned to the coffee shop.

After he was gone, Winnie stood by her car and said a little prayer. Whether Mission Reignite was a success or a dud was out of her hands.

But not out of God's.

Presley

Why had she said yes? Presley knew that Trent meant well, but it was a mistake to go out with him this evening. He'd convinced her that he'd found a quiet, out-of-the-way place with a casual atmosphere, but to be seen with Trent on Valentine's Day would make people assume that they were a couple.

The alternative, though, was even worse. She'd contemplated stocking up on assorted snacks, ordering a pizza, and crashing on her bed with all her favorite romantic comedies queued up to play one after the other and a box of tissues by her side.

Trent, having experience with younger sisters suffering from heartbreak, had obviously sensed what she planned. When she'd admitted he was right, he made her laugh so hard at his imitation of a love-forsaken romantic holed up in an attic bedroom that she'd needed that box of tissues after all.

"Jeans and boots," Trent had said. "Bring a sweater or a jacket. It might get chilly." But that was all he would say about his plans for the evening no matter how much she questioned him.

So that was what she was wearing. An ombré teal sweater over dark boot-cut jeans and black ankle boots with lace insets. Her black denim jacket draped over her arm.

By the time Presley was ready to leave her room, she'd discovered that she was looking forward to the evening with Trent. They'd have fun, they'd laugh, and she'd always have the memory of spending one Valentine's Day with a famous football player.

"You look lovely. As always," Trent said as she descended the stairs. He stood at the bottom of the curving staircase, one hand resting on the banister's newel post. "Are you ready for a special night?"

Presley stopped on the first stair to better match his height and met his gaze. Trent was much more than an attractive athlete. He was personable and easygoing, and he exuded confidence. But despite all his wonderful qualities, that indefinable spark didn't exist between them. It hadn't been there for any man Presley had met or dated.

Not since Clint.

"I'm ready," she said brightly. "Are you going to tell me now where we're going?"

"You'll see soon enough," Trent said. "Hope you're hungry."

"Did you charter a boat?" That notion had come to her when she was trying to decide what to do with her hair. The idea made sense. On a boat they'd have privacy, and she'd definitely need a jacket to ward off the chill of the evening wind. She'd finally decided to leave her hair down but stuck a scrunchie in her pocket in case she needed it.

"No questions." He held up a warning finger. "You simply need to trust me. Will you do that?"

"I don't think I have a choice," Presley said.

Trent checked his watch and grinned. "We're right on time."

He held out his arm, and Presley hesitated only a second before taking it. He led her out the front door and around the veranda to the rear of the property.

She veered toward the parking lot, but he ushered her toward the woods.

"Where are we going?" Presley asked, her mind racing with possibilities. "To the sundial?"

"What was that message again?" Trent asked. "'*Ultima latet*' something."

"'*Ultima latet ut observentur omnes*,'" Presley answered, deliberately pronouncing each word.

He nodded. "It's easier in English. 'Our last hour is hidden from us, so that we watch them all.' If I remember right, we agreed that meant to be watchful and purposeful."

"If I remember right, I told you I didn't excel in philosophy." Neither had she expected a walk through the grounds. Her curiosity—as well as her dread—deepened.

"Me either," he said. "But I've been giving that sundial slogan a lot of thought. There's wisdom in those words."

"Which you've already taken to heart," Presley said.

He raised his eyebrows. "How so?"

"You have this amazing career, but you're *watchful* that something could happen to end it. So you are being *purposeful* in making wise investments and planning your future."

"I hadn't thought of it like that. But I guess it's true." Trent gave a self-satisfied smile. "You've paid me a fine compliment." He left the path and headed toward the three sisters.

"The sundial is that way," Presley reminded him as she motioned in the right direction.

"We're not going to the sundial," he said.

"But you said we were."

"Actually, I didn't. You assumed."

Presley swallowed the forlorn sigh that bubbled inside her. "You're taking me to the climbing tree." She slowed her steps. "I don't want to spend Valentine's Day there. I can't."

Trent stopped and turned to her. "I realize we don't know each other very well, but in the past few days we've shared a lot of secrets."

"I know." More secrets than she should have. Somehow pouring her heart out to a friendly stranger had seemed safe. Once they returned to New York and to their separate lives, they probably wouldn't see each other very often. If at all. They might plan to meet for coffee or to share a pizza, but in time, the frequency of getting together, of staying in contact, would lessen.

"Then trust me," he said. "I wouldn't intentionally do anything to hurt you. And I know how much the climbing tree means to you. But maybe it's time for it to mean something more. The tree is gone, but what's left can still be a special place for you."

"I suppose you're right," Presley said, but she still couldn't move.

"Everything's been arranged," Trent assured her. "No one will be taking our photos and posting them online. Only a handful of people know where we are."

Her guard went up, and the ache in the pit of her stomach deepened. "Who knows?"

"Winnie Bennett and a group of her friends."

Presley frowned. "Why would they know?"

"They're taking care of the food." He tilted his head toward the three sisters. "Shall we go see what's on the menu?"

Presley nodded.

Trent took her hand and escorted her through the copse to the stump.

Lanterns hung from shepherd's hooks stuck in the ground and in the branches of a few of the nearby trees. A cloth covered the stump, which was surrounded by thick cushions. A nearby trolley held a cooler, a tote, and a bucket of drinks. Bouquets of pink and white roses tied with silver ribbon decorated the stump and the trolley.

The scene took Presley's breath away. Her favorite spot, marred by circumstances beyond her control, had been transformed. This was the memory of the climbing tree she'd carry back to New York with her. "Oh, it's beautiful. Like a magical, secret garden."

"Do you like it?" Trent asked.

She squeezed his hand. "I love it."

"I have one more surprise," he said. "But you need to close your eyes."

"Do I have to?" she asked.

"Yes, you have to." Trent let go of her hand and smiled. "And no peeking."

After Presley covered her eyes, she sensed Trent stepping away. A rustling sounded. Footsteps.

"You can open them now," someone said.

Presley opened her eyes, and her hands went from her eyes to her mouth.

Clint was standing directly in front of her.

A million questions raced through her mind. But she couldn't form the words to ask any of them. To say anything.

Clint cleared his throat. "Hello, Presley."

"Hello," Presley said, her voice shaking. She noticed that his features had matured, become more angular. But in his eyes and in his hesitant smile were traces of the boy she'd once known.

For a moment they stood silent, taking each other in, and it seemed the years peeled away. They were eighteen again. The future, glorious and beckoning, was waiting for them to step into its light.

"I have something for you." Clint reached into his pocket, then held out his closed fist. His left fist. His ring finger was bare.

The butterflies in her stomach dipped and swooped and made her dizzy. "You're not married," Presley whispered.

He lowered his hand but kept his fist closed. "Today was supposed to be my wedding day, but we called off the engagement months ago."

"I'm sorry." It seemed the appropriate thing to say, but she wasn't sorry. Not really.

"Don't be." Clint smiled. "I'm not. Especially not now."

Presley didn't know how to respond.

"I've missed you," he said. "All these years, it's been like a piece of my heart has been walking around without me."

Could this moment truly be happening? Did he still love her? "It's been like that for me too."

"Then why didn't you call me?" Clint asked. "Why didn't you respond to my messages?"

How could she explain how difficult it had been to stay away from him? "At first, I didn't have a choice. Mother wouldn't allow it. She threatened and demanded and . . ." Presley tensed as the horrible memories of those days washed over her. "I wasn't strong enough to stand up to her."

She'd been a coward and too young to muster the strength she needed. But she wouldn't be a coward now. Clint deserved to know the truth.

Presley took a deep breath. "I realized Mother was right. Not what she did—that was wrong. But we both still had some growing up to do. And later, I didn't think you'd want to hear from me." She clasped her hands together. "Can you ever forgive me?"

Clint held out his hand again and opened his fingers. A silver thimble rested in his palm. "Do you know what this is?"

She gasped as she reached for the token. Clint wasn't married. He wasn't getting married. And he was offering her . . . "A kiss."

Clint took a step closer and wrapped her fingers around the thimble. "Will you give me back the thimble?"

Presley threw her arms around his neck. Her eyes spoke her answer a moment before her lips pressed against his. He tasted of spring breezes and summer sunshine, of days long gone and a future that still waited for them. She loved him. She'd always loved him.

And she'd never leave him again.

Clint

Clint's heart melted as the tender warmth of their kiss awakened the love he'd always felt for Presley. Why had he let her leave without a fight? Because he'd been barely eighteen. Insecure. And more hurt by her abrupt departure than he'd ever been hurt before. But now he understood. Presley had been hurting too.

He didn't want to let her go, but he ended the kiss and touched his forehead to hers. "Happy Valentine's Day."

"Happy Valentine's Day," Presley whispered.

He gestured toward the stump. "Winnie and her friends made us food. I hope you're hungry."

Her face reddened, and she glanced around the clearing. "Where's Trent?"

"He shook my hand and left while your eyes were still closed." Clint intertwined their fingers. "I've got something to show you." He led her to the stump and motioned for her to take a seat.

Presley settled onto one of the cushions and tucked her feet beneath her.

"I heard you've been searching for this." Clint retrieved a rusted metal box from the bottom shelf of the trolley and placed it on her lap.

"Our memory box," she said. "It's why I came back."

"I noticed the holes you dug up," Clint said as he sat beside her. "Why didn't you ask me for it?"

"I thought you were married. Or at least engaged." Presley hung her head and touched the top of the box. "And after the way I left you, I wasn't sure you'd ever want to see me again."

"That's all I ever wanted." Clint had tried to convince himself that wasn't true. He'd even almost convinced himself he was in love with someone else. At least his engagement to Margot had ended. If it hadn't . . . There was no need to wallow in what-ifs. He and Presley were together now. Nothing else mattered.

Presley raised her eyes to his, and the love in her gaze almost did him in. "Will you forgive me?" she asked.

"There's nothing to forgive." Clint brushed her hair from her shoulder and tucked her beneath his arm. "I know it's six months early, but why don't we go ahead and open the box?"

"You haven't opened it yet?" she asked, obviously surprised.

"Without you?" He smiled. "Never."

30

Grace

Grace, wearing a long-sleeved midnight-blue dress with a gold necklace, paused as she entered the barn. Though much of the building was shrouded in darkness, one corner was softly lit with shaded lamps and candles.

Billowy white curtains formed a backdrop around a table for two covered in a snow-white tablecloth and adorned with red cloth napkins and a matching red runner. A gorgeous floral centerpiece was flanked by white candles. Sterling silver tableware lay next to white plates resting on silver platters. Red and silver ribbons tied the white cloth covering the two chairs. Soft music sounded from hidden speakers. The ambience was perfect.

Happiness for her sister warmed Grace from the inside. Charlotte's romantic heart would appreciate the attention to detail and the intimacy The Busy Bees had managed to create. Grace couldn't wait for Charlotte and Dean to arrive.

A shuffling sound came from behind one of the curtains.

"Winnie?" Grace called out. "Is that you?"

The curtain moved, and Winston trotted over to her, sporting a red bow tie.

"Oh, Winston, you're adorable," Grace said.

Then Spencer stepped from behind the curtain and into the light.

Grace almost gasped. Wearing a gray suit with a silver tie, he appeared as fine and distinguished as any man she'd ever seen. "What are you doing here?" she blurted out.

"I'm hoping to have a romantic Valentine's Day dinner with the loveliest woman in South Carolina." He extended a red rose. "That is, if you'll join me."

"But this dinner . . ." She pressed her lips together. "It's for Charlotte and Dean."

Spencer closed the gap between them and reached for her hand. "No, this dinner is for us."

"I don't understand. Winnie told me to come and play hostess for Charlotte and Dean and take some photos."

"It was a ruse." Spencer led her to the table, Winston on their heels. "But don't worry. Charlotte and Dean will have their dinner too." He grinned and tilted his head to the opposite corner of the barn. "Over there and closer to midnight."

He pulled out her chair, and Grace smoothed her dress as she sat down. Her heart raced as she tried to make sense of what was happening.

Winston plopped down at her feet, watching her with bright eyes.

Grace inhaled the fragrance from the lovely rose. "You planned all this?"

"With a lot of help," Spencer admitted, taking the seat across from her. "First I talked to Charlotte, and then we discussed it with Winnie. She brought in The Busy Bees. They've been here for a couple of hours getting everything prepared."

"It's all so beautiful. And so unexpected." Though perhaps she should have suspected something was up from the way Winnie had been acting the last couple of days.

"I'm sorry I haven't been around much this week. I was afraid I'd say the wrong thing and spoil the whole surprise." Spencer stretched his hand across the table. "You were surprised, weren't you?"

"Absolutely." She placed her hand in his. "And very touched."

He squeezed her fingers. "Happy Valentine's Day, Grace."

31

Presley

At first, Presley didn't think she could eat a bite. Her stomach was too tied up in knots from seeing Clint.

But sorting through the items in their memory box and reminiscing about their childhood summers shifted the relationship between them. They'd found the tickets from the time they'd gone to a concert in Charleston. The American flags came from one summer's Fourth of July celebration held on the lakeshore. Beneath the photo of Presley that Clint had added when he'd retrieved the box, they found the acorn button and the original thimble.

The embarrassment and discomfort of seeing each other for the first time in almost ten years had faded. The inexplicable bond that connected them before connected them once again.

After they'd returned their treasures to the memory box, including the thimble Winnie had given Clint, Presley reluctantly closed the lid. It made a small click. But the click didn't represent an ending or a closure. Instead, the tiny sound comforted, like the ticking of a familiar clock. Or the quiet beat of Clint's heart when she rested her head against his chest.

"Winnie and her friends will be disappointed if we don't eat," Clint said. "Are you hungry?"

"Not really," she said. Too many unanswered questions remained between them. They were friends again. But their lives had taken such different paths. Clint's engagement, he'd told her, had ended when he refused to move to California with his fiancée. Presley couldn't expect him to move to New York. Which meant—if they were to have a future together—she'd need to return to Magnolia Harbor.

Perhaps it was too soon to think of that possibility. Probably way too soon. But the mere idea sent a joyful tremor up her spine.

"Winnie promised me a French silk pie if I showed up this evening," Clint remarked as he uncovered a round dish. "And here it is."

"Wait a minute." Presley pretended to glare at him. "She bribed you to meet me?"

Clint swiped his finger through the whipped cream topping. "Let's just say the pie was the frosting on the cake." He grinned. "Even though it was the whipped cream on the pie."

"Are you sticking with that story?" she teased.

"It's the only one I got." He opened the lid on the cooler. "Let's see what we have here. Looks like thinly sliced meat and all the fixings. Smoked turkey and roast beef. And of course, honey-baked ham."

"Of course." Honey-baked ham had been its own food group for Presley's grandparents. Grandma often sent Presley and Clint out the door with thick ham sandwiches wrapped in oversize cotton napkins. Another memory she'd tucked away and almost forgotten until her return.

A memory that made her stomach growl. Thankfully, it was too low for Clint to hear. She unzipped the tote. "Here's the bread. Wraps and hoagie rolls. And little bags of chips." Her stomach rumbled again, louder this time, and she winced.

"Wow." Clint grinned and handed her a plate. "Glad to know you still have an appetite. Do you remember that time we went to the county fair—"

"And gorged on funnel cakes and candied apples," Presley interrupted with a laugh. "How could I forget?"

"You got cotton candy stuck in your hair," he said.

"At least I didn't spill lemonade on my pants."

"I didn't spill it," Clint insisted. "You bumped me."

"*You* bumped *me*. That's how I got cotton candy in my hair."

His broad smile crinkled his eyes. "You looked cute with your hair all gummed up like that."

"And you looked pitiable when your pants got wet." Presley paused as she split open her roll, reliving the memory. "But that didn't stop you from having a good time. Remember what you did?"

"Went to the fair office, borrowed a pair of scissors, and turned those pants into shorts." Clint shrugged while layering slices of roast beef, ham, and Swiss cheese on his sandwich. "It wasn't a big deal."

"To some people it would have been." The incident had stuck with her all these years because it had meant something. They'd been only about twelve or thirteen. But Clint's fix-it attitude had appealed to her. There hadn't been many people in her life with that kind of resourcefulness. "I would have gone home to change."

"If I'd gone home, I would have missed spending time with you," Clint said quietly. "That's all I wanted to do back then."

"Me too," Presley said. She realized that didn't come out right and rushed to explain. "I mean, I didn't want to spend time with me. I wanted to spend time with you."

Clint didn't respond. He lowered his gaze while spreading spicy brown mustard on his sandwich.

The air between them had shifted again. Presley focused on arranging the lettuce leaves and tomato slices on top of the chipotle Gouda cheese she'd added to her turkey sandwich.

They both grabbed bags of chips, then settled on the cushions.

"Do you mind if I bless the food?" Clint asked.

"I'd like that," she said.

He twined his fingers with hers, and they bowed their heads.

"Our Father in heaven, we thank You for the Valentine's Day You've given us," Clint said. "For bringing us together again. And for Winnie and the other ladies who cared enough about us to provide this food. Especially the French silk pie."

Presley tried to stifle a sudden bout of the giggles but didn't quite succeed.

"Shh." Clint playfully nudged her. "Amen."

"Amen," she echoed.

"You should take praying more seriously." He opened one of the sodas and handed it to her.

She shivered as the curved glass bottle chilled her hand. "Me?"

"Hey, French silk pie is my favorite. You bet I'm thankful for it."

Presley sipped her soda. His favorite pie used to be lemon meringue. When had that changed? What else about him had changed? They weren't the same people they'd been before. She couldn't deny that fact.

"Did you mean what you said?" Clint's somber tone broke into her reverie.

"What did I say?"

"That you wanted to spend time with me. Back when we were kids."

"I meant it," she said without hesitation.

Clint nodded slowly as if he were deep in thought. Or perhaps choosing what to say next. He took a long sip of his drink, draining half the bottle. "What about now?" He didn't look at her but focused straight ahead. "Do you want to spend time with me now?"

Presley followed his gaze. In the dim lighting provided by the torches, the three sisters formed a dark outline against the darker sky. His question was simple. And yet deeper than the deepest part of Lake Haven. Presley glanced up, where the moon and stars played hide-and-seek behind the clouds.

Beyond them was Neverland, a fictional place where lost boys fought with pirates and mermaids sang in the lagoon. Where Wendy tended their hurts and told them bedtime stories. Where thimbles were kisses and an acorn button saved the Wendy bird's life from an arrow. An imaginary land where children didn't grow up.

When Mother whisked her away, Presley had longed to fly to such a place. But only if Clint was there too.

She rested her head against his shoulder. "More than anything."

"I can't leave Donnie."

Again, simple words with depths and layers. "I know."

A long silence passed between them, the sandwiches and chips forgotten. Their fingers found each other, linked together.

"Life in Magnolia Harbor isn't as exciting as it is in New York," Clint said, breaking the quiet.

Presley straightened and shifted on the cushion so she could look into his eyes. "What do you know of life in New York?"

He shrugged. "What I see on TV."

"It is exciting. And vibrant and inspiring." One corner of her mouth tilted up while the other tilted down. The expression Grandpa laughingly called her happy-sad face. "But it's also competitive and challenging. Sometimes not in a good way."

"Your designing dreams came true there." A guilty expression flitted across his face. "I searched your name after I saw you at the movies the other night. Something I'd avoided doing all these years." He heaved a deep sigh as he played with her fingers. "I read all about your success. About the Ingram Flair. I can't ask you to give that up."

His final words punched her chest. In the deep place of her heart she wanted—hoped—Clint would ask her to return. But then the words settled into a clarifying truth.

"It's true. You can't." If he did, Presley would once again be following someone else's wishes instead of making her own decisions. The comparison between Clint asking her to leave New York and Mother's demand that she leave Magnolia Harbor was shaky. But such a request would be motivated by the same thing as Mother's demand.

Love.

And, Presley had to admit, in Mother's case an unhealthy amount of control.

"Then what do we do?" he asked.

"We eat our sandwiches and that lovely pie," she answered. "We get to know each other again. And we pray."

"I like that plan." His tender smile and the affection in his eyes caused her stomach to flip.

Presley summoned all her willpower to keep from throwing her arms around his neck and kissing those tantalizing lips.

Her willpower didn't listen.

32

Grace

Grace and Spencer lingered over their leisurely dinner, unobtrusively served by Winnie and Gus. As they were enjoying servings of pomegranate sorbet, served in crystal dishes, Dean arrived with a covered dish.

"Looks like I'm right on time," Dean said, his brown eyes sparkling. "I brought your dessert."

Grace pressed her hand against her stomach. The meal had been absolutely delicious, and she wasn't sure she could eat anything else. But Dean had made whatever hid beneath that cover. Which meant it was sure to be delectable. "What did you bring us?" she asked.

Before Dean could answer, Winnie and Gus appeared from behind the curtain.

"You're just in time for the reveal," Dean said to them as he set the dish on a trolley near the table. "Happy Valentine's Day to one of my favorite competitors in the lodging business"—he bowed to Grace—"and a close friend." He nodded at Spencer. "And now, without further ado . . ." He lifted the cover with a flourish to reveal two individual servings. "Chocolate torte with salted ganache and raspberries."

Grace drank in the sight of the scrumptious dessert. "I didn't think I could eat another bite, but this is irresistible."

"The finest compliment a chef could receive," Dean said.

Winnie cleared away the sorbet dishes, Gus refilled water glasses, and Dean served the torte.

"Dean?" Charlotte walked toward them from the barn entrance. She wore a stunning pale-pink dress with a high neckline, flouncy skirt, and cut-out shoulders. Silver drop earrings and strappy heels completed her ensemble. She glanced from him to Winnie and back again. "What are you doing here?"

Dean beamed with pride. "I brought dessert for Grace and Spencer."

"Looks delicious." Charlotte wrapped her arm around his waist, and he drew her into a side hug. "I didn't know you were going to be here. I'm supposed to sing a romantic song or two."

Grace caught her sister's gaze. "We'd love to hear you sing, but I think our beloved aunt has other plans for you and Dean."

"I do," Winnie said. "Dean, thank you so much for bringing the dessert. But I asked you to bring it because Grace wanted to do something special for you and Charlotte."

"You planned this?" Charlotte asked Grace.

"All the credit goes to Winnie and The Busy Bees," Grace replied. "And Gus."

"Let's not forget Gus," Spencer said with a laugh. "If you ever need a waiter at The Tidewater, Dean, you might want to give Gus a call."

"No thanks." Gus chuckled. "I'm retired and plan to stay that way. The only person I plan to wait on is this lovely lady right here." He put his arm around Winnie's shoulders and kissed her cheek. "Happy Valentine's Day, darling."

Winnie blushed. "Let's leave these two to finish their dinner." She turned to Charlotte and Dean. "And get these two started on theirs." She waved her hand toward the other end of the barn. "Lights, please."

Gus flipped a few switches. In an opposite corner, soft lighting appeared, revealing another private table set for two.

"If you'll follow me," Gus said in a grand voice.

Dean caught Charlotte's gaze and held out his arm. "Shall we?"

Charlotte turned to Grace, a broad smile lighting up her face. "Happy Valentine's Day."

"Happy Valentine's Day to you too," Grace said.

Charlotte took Dean's arm, and they followed Gus to their table.

After Winnie disappeared behind the curtain, Grace focused her attention on Spencer. "I can't thank you enough for this evening. Everything was perfect."

"It's not over yet." He took her hand in his. "When we're finished with dessert, will you join me in a moonlit walk?"

Grace's pulse raced. "I'd love to."

33

Clint

Without a doubt, this was the best Valentine's Day ever. Clint would choose a picnic at the climbing tree stump with Presley over a fancy wedding and reception any day. Who was he kidding? He'd choose scrubbing floors if Presley was there to embrace him when he finished.

The grandfather clock chimed the quarter hour as they entered the kitchen. A light shone above the sink, and Clint switched on the pendants over the island.

"It's almost midnight." Presley set the tote with the leftover bread and chips on the counter. "What are we supposed to do with the rest of the food?"

"Winnie said to put the cold stuff back in the fridge and leave the rest on the counter," he answered.

Presley slipped off her jacket and rubbed her arms. "I didn't realize how chilly it had gotten until we started walking back."

"That's because we were keeping each other warm." Clint laughed as Presley's cheeks turned crimson. "Hey, there's nothing wrong with good old-fashioned kissing. In fact, I think it's nice."

"Me too." Presley giggled.

How he'd missed that beautiful sound and her easy blushes. As they'd sat under the stars and enjoyed their sandwiches and pie, nothing was actually settled between them. But somehow Clint knew deep inside that God meant them for each other. He always had.

Whether that plan had been waylaid by Presley's domineering mother or whether their separation was part of the overall plan, he didn't know. But it no longer mattered. They were together again, and together they'd figure out their future.

Clint stashed the mustard jar and similar condiments in the refrigerator. "All done."

"I took care of our trash," she said.

They stared at each other across the island. Presley's dark hair, disheveled from the night breeze, hung below her shoulders. Her lipstick had faded, but her mouth was still a delightful shade of pink. She couldn't be more beautiful if she'd been all dressed up with every hair in its proper place.

"What are you thinking?" she asked.

"How much I don't want this day to end."

"Me either." A playful tone brightened her voice. "And yet it must, or we'll be standing in this kitchen for eternity."

"I can think of worse places," Clint said.

"We could at least go to the living room," Presley suggested. "Unless you need to get home."

"I choose living room." He rounded the island and grabbed her hand.

As they headed toward the living room, the notes from the piano in the music room grew louder.

"Who do you suppose is playing this late?" he asked.

"There's only one way to find out."

They stopped in the doorway to the music room, quietly listening as the pianist played "As Time Goes By."

When the final note ended, Presley clapped and entered the room. Clint followed her.

"That was lovely, Trent," she said. "I didn't know you played."

"My one and only hidden talent." He shifted on the seat and nodded at Clint. "How was your evening? Or do I even need to ask?"

"Unforgettable," Presley said, resting her hands on the piano.

Clint stood behind her, his arm around her waist. "Thanks for making sure she came out there," he said.

"Anytime, man." Trent shifted back to the piano and flexed his fingers. "'Unforgettable,' huh? I know that one."

As he played the Nat King Cole classic, Presley leaned into Clint. He couldn't see her face, but he sensed that her eyes were closed.

The woman he'd loved since childhood nestled against him, and Clint knew that he would hold this moment in his heart for the rest of his life.

34

Winnie

After serving beet carpaccio topped with crumbled goat cheese and arugula to Charlotte and Dean, Winnie and Gus returned to the serving station behind the curtain.

Gus stifled a yawn. "I can't remember the last time I was up this late. It's Saturday morning, you know."

"Only by a few minutes." Winnie plucked fresh thyme to garnish the coq au vin. "I'm tired too. But did you see how delighted both of our nieces looked tonight? I wish Hazel could have been here. She would have loved an evening like this." A lump formed in her throat, and the back of her eyes stung. "If she could have seen her beautiful daughters . . . Oh, Gus, we are so blessed to live close to Grace and Charlotte."

Gus wrapped Winnie in a hug. "Now, now. No tears. I know you miss Hazel. So do I. But even though it's past midnight, I'm going to declare that Valentine's Day isn't over until I taste the strawberry cheesecake you made for me and we've had at least a few hours of sleep. And I'm not going to bed until I've had a dance with my forever valentine."

His familiar voice, his words, and his gentle touch warmed Winnie's heart. They'd been high school sweethearts, and their love had only grown through their years of marriage. She would never have wanted to experience the joys and trials of life with anyone else by her side, and she knew with every fiber of her being that Gus felt the same way about her. On the rare occasion when love seemed to falter, respect for one another filled in the gap.

"How about that dance?" Gus whispered.

Grace

Moonlight shimmered on the gentle waves lapping against Lake Haven's shore. Grace and Spencer stood on the dock and gazed across the water toward The Tidewater. Though the restaurant had closed for the evening, its discreet security lights spotlighted the lake's opposite bank. A slight breeze carried the rhythmic chirrups and bellows of nocturnal creatures. The perfect background music for a perfect evening.

When they'd left the barn, Spencer had settled his jacket around Grace's shoulders. Now she clasped the front together against the night chill. Spencer stood beside her, his arm loose around her waist.

"Such a beautiful night," Grace murmured.

"The temperature is supposed to drop tomorrow." His light-blue eyes sparkled with mischief. "I thought we could take out the kayaks for another unseasonable adventure. Are you game?"

"I hope you're teasing," she answered. "Though I should challenge you to another race since you cheated last time."

Spencer raised his eyebrows. "Me? Cheat?"

"Yes, you." Grace poked him with her finger. "You're a cheater."

"Now we definitely have to get out the kayaks," he said.

Grace shivered as a gust of wind swept across the back of her neck. "I have an idea. Why don't we plan a seasonable adventure instead?"

"What do you have in mind?" he asked.

"Oh, I don't know," she said playfully. "Maybe an activity that doesn't involve the frigid water."

"Where would be the fun in that?" Spencer joked as he pulled two slips of paper from his back pocket. "Perhaps you'd be interested in these."

Grace had to admit that he'd definitely piqued her curiosity. "What are they?"

"Two tickets." He waved them in front of her, but it was too dark to read the writing on them.

Gracious, the man could be so maddening. Thank goodness he was handsome. The moonlight seemed to seek out the silver in his salt-and-pepper hair, and his teasing smile tugged at Grace's heart. But he didn't need to know that. At least not yet.

Her tone matched his playful banter. "To . . . ?"

"Something indoors," Spencer said.

"Tell me."

He laughed and stuck the tickets into the outer pocket of his suit. "You can see them later. And if you're willing and can get away from the inn for a few hours tomorrow, then give me a call."

"You're being very mysterious," Grace remarked.

Spencer laughed again, a soft laugh that made her smile.

They'd been friends, good friends, since he moved to Blossom Hill Farm. But tonight's romantic dinner had shifted their relationship into uncharted territory. The flutters in Grace's stomach exhilarated her. And, truth be told, they frightened her.

Her expression must have changed because Spencer's did too. The smile faded, and his eyes no longer danced. Instead, they held her in a spell she didn't want to break.

"Do you like mysterious?" he asked.

The question caught her off guard. Did she? Grace turned and stared across the lake as she considered her answer. Muddled thoughts swirled inside her. How her parents had thought of her as the responsible one, the calm in the eye of the storm. Typical firstborn. Striving to do the right thing, to organize and plan the smallest details of any undertaking. To arrange her life so that she could handle the hardships without falling apart.

That was what she'd had to do when her husband died unexpectedly. She'd had no choice but to be strong both for her sake and for their son. But that had been more than twenty years ago. Since then she'd achieved success in her marketing career, found the courage to leave the security of a corporate position, and opened a bed-and-breakfast with her sister.

"Grace?"

She gazed into his eyes, so mesmerizing, so filled with tenderness and longing and hope that her breath caught in her throat. Dare she take that step toward love? Could she risk her heart again?

"Yes," she breathed. "I like mysterious."

Spencer smiled as he drew her closer.

She rested one hand on his chest. His heart beat a pulsing rhythm beneath her palm.

Her gaze didn't waver from his until he glanced at her lips. Anticipation surged through her, and she closed her eyes as his mouth covered hers.

She slid both arms around his neck as his arms encircled her, holding her tight as they indulged in the wonder, in the mystery, of their first kiss.

Grace

A soft knock sounded at her bedroom door.

Grace glanced up from her book and checked the clock. It was 1:37 a.m. Who in the world could that be?

Winston lifted his head from his cushioned doggy bed.

The knock sounded again followed by a stage whisper. "Grace? Are you awake?"

Charlotte.

She should have guessed. "Come in."

The door opened, and Charlotte slipped inside before closing it behind her. She'd loosened her hair and changed from her pink dress into jeans and a sweater. "I'm so glad you're awake." She practically hopped onto Grace's bed.

Winston jumped up beside her.

"I couldn't sleep," Grace said as she placed a marker in her book.

Charlotte's eyes shimmered with excitement. "Did you have a wonderful time with Spencer this evening?"

A spontaneous smile curved Grace's lips, and she lowered her eyes. The memory of Spencer's tender embrace, the warmth and thrill of their kiss, was too new—too fresh—to share with anyone else. Even Charlotte. But she couldn't hide her bliss from her sister's sharp notice.

"Obviously you did." Charlotte smiled. "I'm so glad. This was the best Valentine's Day ever."

"I agree." Grace set the book on her nightstand and hugged her knees. "Were you surprised?"

"Blown away." Charlotte sat cross-legged on the bed and cuddled Winston. "I loved the wooden heart Angel made. It's engraved with our names and the date."

"It's beautiful," Grace said.

"Winnie outdid herself, and Gus was so cute," Charlotte continued. "When we left, they were still dancing."

"May we always be as young at heart as the two of them," Grace said.

"I hope so." Charlotte released a deep sigh. "Thanks for all you did to make this a night to remember."

"I can't take any credit. Winnie mobilized The Busy Bees." Grace frowned. "I'm only sorry your dinner had to be so late. You and Dean didn't have as much time together as Spencer and I did."

"Not to worry," Charlotte said. "We're extending our Valentine's Day to a Sunday dinner in Charleston. That is, if you don't mind handling the hospitality hour that night. I'll have the food ready before I leave."

No way could Grace refuse the pleading in her sister's eyes. "I'm happy to take care of it. Especially if you'll do a favor for me."

"Name it."

Grace opened her nightstand drawer and pulled out the two tickets that Spencer had tucked into his suit jacket. He'd insisted on leaving them with her when they said a final—and lingering—good night on the veranda outside the dining room. Which reminded her . . . "Guess who was in the music room when we came back."

"Must have been a guest." Charlotte's eyes lit up. "Oh, I know. Presley and Trent."

"You're half right."

"Which half?"

"Presley," Grace replied. "She was with Clint Calloway."

"The landscape designer?" Charlotte asked. "With Presley Ingram, the fashion designer? How did they even meet? What were they doing?"

Grace laughed at the onslaught of questions. "Yes. Yes. I have no idea. Playing a game."

"A game?" Charlotte repeated. "I don't understand."

"Neither do I. But from the way they looked at each other . . ." Grace shrugged. "I got the sense they didn't want the evening to end. For all I know, they're still out there."

"I don't think so. The only light I saw burning was yours." Charlotte shook her head. "Presley and Clint. Wasn't he engaged to somebody in town?"

Trust Charlotte not to be current on the local gossip. "That ended months ago."

"Do you think Presley knows?" Charlotte asked. "I really hoped that she would hit it off with Trent. I mean, they've gone out almost every night they've been here."

"I guess we can never know where our hearts will take us."

"Except in your case." Charlotte's eyes twinkled in the dim lighting. "It seems to me that your heart took you straight to Spencer."

Grace smiled. "And yours took you straight to Dean."

"We're so blessed," Charlotte said. "Would you have ever guessed when we opened this place that we'd experience a night like tonight?"

"No." The night had been more special than Grace could have ever hoped for. "I never would have."

"I guess I should say good night." Charlotte rose from the bed. "Wait a minute. Weren't you going to ask me for a favor?"

"I need to be away for a few hours tomorrow." Grace laughed. "I mean, this afternoon." She handed the tickets to Charlotte. "Spencer gave me these."

"'Charleston Historical Society's Step-Back-in-Time Trivia Contest and Wine-Tasting Extravaganza,'" Charlotte read. She beamed. "I'll cover things here. You go have a great time. This one's definitely a date."

Grace laughed. "No doubt about it."

37

Presley

How could Presley have overslept? Today of all days!

Maybe because she'd been up until the wee hours of the morning. After Trent finished playing "Unforgettable," he'd left Presley and Clint alone in the music room. Reluctant to say goodbye to each other, they'd played a board game. It seemed to take forever because they kept stopping between turns to talk. After all, nearly ten years of catching up couldn't take place in only a few hours.

Today they were going to visit with Donnie at Hope Shelter to give him and Presley a chance to get reacquainted, then take him to lunch at Aunt Patsy's Porch. But first Presley needed to talk to Grace and Charlotte.

As soon as she was showered and dressed, she headed for the lobby. Breakfast was over, but a few dishes remained on the table. She carried them into the kitchen. "Knock, knock. Mind if I help?"

Grace turned from the sink. She appeared tired but happy. She pointed to the counter. "Just set those over there if you don't mind. Can I fix you something? There's juice and fruit. And a few leftover pastries."

Presley set the plates where Grace had indicated and eyed the tray of pastries and breads. "Is it okay if I take the last honey muffin?"

"Absolutely." Grace placed a clean plate and napkin in front of her. "Coffee? Hot chocolate?"

"No thanks." Presley placed the muffin on her plate and heaved a sigh. She couldn't put this off any longer. "I want to apologize."

Grace gave her a quizzical look. "For what?"

Winnie must not have told her niece about Presley's vandalism. "I'm the one who dug the holes around the climbing tree. I mean, the grandfather stump."

Grace was silent for a moment, and Presley wanted to melt under her steady gaze.

"Are you sure you don't want anything to drink?" Grace finally asked.

Surprised by the question, Presley stammered over her answer. "M-maybe some juice?"

"The climbing tree?" Grace poured orange juice into a glass and gave it to Presley, then took a seat at the island. "I can see why someone would call it that. But only someone who'd seen it before it was struck by lightning."

"I haven't been honest with you," Presley admitted. "This house belonged to my grandparents. And my great-grandparents. And so on."

Grace's eyes widened. "Why didn't you tell us?"

"It's hard to explain. I guess you could say I came back to dig up the past. I thought that was the only way to bury it." Presley shook her head. "I know that doesn't make any sense."

"Did you find what you were searching for?" Grace asked.

"Yes. Just not there." Presley crumbled the muffin into pieces. "I was going to try to cover the holes back up, but then Winnie found me. Anyway, I'll take care of the expense. Not me, exactly. Clint said he'd square things with Oliver."

"Clint Calloway?" Grace gave a knowing nod. "You two know each other."

"I used to spend summers here with my grandparents," she said, and the story came spilling out.

Grace listened with motherly compassion. She asked all the right questions, said all the right things. Most importantly, she wasn't mad about the holes.

Presley ended her story with another apology. "I'm sorry again for deceiving you."

"You're forgiven." Grace's compassionate smile eased Presley's guilt. "What are you going to do now?"

"I'd like to stay here another week or so. If the Wisteria Loft Suite isn't already booked."

"Not until the end of the month," Grace said. "You're not in any hurry to return to New York?"

"No hurry at all." Presley grinned. "Charlotte promised I could help with her hot chocolate experiments. We haven't had a chance to do that yet."

"*That's* your reason for staying?" Grace asked.

"Maybe." Presley gave a teasing laugh. Her heart felt lighter, more at ease, than it had in a long time. As if all the happiness of her childhood summers was once again hers. "I do love hot chocolate."

Presley found Trent coming down the stairs with his luggage. "I thought you weren't flying home until tomorrow," she said.

"That was the plan," he said. "But I got a call this morning from a couple of buddies who are headed to Florida for a deep-sea fishing expedition. It sounded like fun, so I'm headed south."

"What about your venture?"

"We've already laid the groundwork," Trent answered. "My partners here will work on negotiating the land purchase, the permits, and so on. And I'll ask my buddies for generous donations while we're out at sea."

"I'd like to help out in some way too," Presley offered. "Please keep me posted."

He gave her a warm smile. "Thanks. I will. So what are you going to do now?"

"I'm staying for at least another week," Presley answered. "You know, to get reacquainted with the area."

"With the area?" Trent asked. "Or with a special person?"

Butterflies danced in her stomach. "Both."

He set down his bag and gave her a bone-crushing hug. "I'm thrilled for you. And I expect an invite to the wedding."

Her cheeks flushed. "If there is one, you can't miss it."

Trent pulled back, and his eyes danced with amusement. "Trust your big brother. There will be one."

Presley walked with him to the door, and they made plans to get together for lunch once they both returned to the city.

After he left, she retrieved her bag and her jacket from her suite, then wandered outside to wait for Clint. The sun seemed to shine brighter than it had all week, and a light breeze stirred the waves of Lake Haven.

Drawn to the scenic view, Presley sat on the edge of the dock and let her feet swing above the lake's cold waters. She closed her eyes and breathed a prayer of gratitude for all the joy and peace that she had experienced since her reunion with Clint. Sunlight warmed her cheeks, and a familiar twitch surged through her fingers.

She took Shiloh's gift from her bag and unzipped the sketch pad.

The future was still a big unknown, and the situation with her colleague remained unresolved. But it could no longer hurt her.

With one of the pencils, she drew quick, sure lines on the thick paper. She smiled. The Ingram Flair was back.

38

Grace

Grace pulled her hair back into a sophisticated ponytail, then examined her reflection in the mirror. The ensemble—a black blouse over a red-and-black plaid skirt with knee-high boots—suited her perfectly. Pleased with her appearance, she smiled. Hopefully, Spencer would be pleased too.

After last night's romantic Valentine's Day dinner, she no longer doubted that their trip to Charleston to see *Les Misérables* was Spencer's attempt at a first date. Perhaps if Charlotte hadn't been peeking through the window, he would have kissed her then.

But it was worth the wait when Spencer kissed her in the moonlight last night. Her sister had given her the best of Valentine's Day gifts without even realizing it.

After one last glance in the mirror, Grace left her private quarters with Winston trotting along beside her. She found Spencer in the dining room staring out the French doors.

"Wishing you were on the lake?" Grace asked.

At the sound of her voice, Spencer turned around. His eyes widened, and an appreciative smile brightened his face. He walked over to her and took both her hands in his. "You look absolutely lovely."

Warmth touched her cheeks as her eyes expressed her gratitude for the compliment. "Thank you. I'm ready to go whenever you are."

Spencer tilted his head toward the doors. "Come look at this first."

They stepped onto the veranda, and Spencer gestured toward the dock. Presley and Clint stood near the edge, their arms around each other's waists and heads tucked together.

"I'm happy for them." Grace sighed contentedly. The Magnolia Harbor Inn had once again worked its magic. "Young love is so sweet."

Spencer pulled her into an embrace. "Grown-up love is too," he whispered.

Yes, it is, Grace thought as Spencer bent to kiss her.